First published in the UK in 2023 By West Avenue Publishing, Peterlee, County Durham.

Heather C Page, Linda M Crate, Jessica Turnbull, Stephen S Power, Sean E Britten, Andrew Murphy, Jason P Burnham, Matias F Travieso, Alex Souza, Mark Mills, Alex Evans, Jibril Stevenson, Joachim Heijndermans, Ismail Ahmad, Dibyasree Nandy, Ben Sawyer, J D Byrne, Mary Jo Rabe, Kathryn Reilly, Rohan Magerman, Oliver Smith, L N Hunter, Marisca Pichette.

ISBN 978-1-7393664-0-7

A FLIGHT OF DRAGONS ANTHOLOGY

West Avenue
Publishing

Most Treasured

By Andrew murphy

Upon entering the vast chamber, the noble knight was taken aback by the sight that lay before him.

He had expected there to be a great treasure hidden within, but nothing like this.

In the center of the cave, the dragon sat resting upon its massive hoard. It gazed up to look at its unexpected guest.

"Impressive, is it not?" The colossal beast inquired without worry.

"I must admit," the knight replied, heavy sword lowered and visor of his helmet lifted so as to better take in what he was seeing, "It is not what I was expecting."

"It has taken me several centuries to procure it all," the dragon replied, "But the time was well spent I think."

With a great clawed hand, it happily showed off the fruits of its labors.

Stepping closer, the knight knelt before the dragon and gazed at the piles and stacks of treasures which seemed to fill every nook and cranny of the great chamber.

No Kings or Queens, nor Lords or Ladies of the land had ever held in their possession riches such as these. Nor could they even conceive of such a thing.

The knight was in awe, unable to find the words to describe

the sight that lay all around him.

Instead, he looked to the dragon and simply asked: "May I read one?"

With a kind smile, the dragon picked up one of the many volumes from a nearby pile of books and handed it to its guest.

"Of course. This one is a personal favorite of mine. Enjoy."

Dragon's Breath

By Heather C Page

Of dragon's breath and dragon's claw,
Gruesome tales pass down, forever more.
At dusk the men depart; blood to spill,
Death lingers slyly in the dragon's lair; the air is still.

Darkness folds in, consumes the dragon's sight,
As day slips carelessly into the black of night.
For those who seek the dragon's fiery wrath,
Must surely tread a treacherous and rocky path.

The dragon defends its hoard, through tooth and through nail,
But his ferocious, fiery efforts are sadly to no avail.
For the dragon is viciously conquered, and duly slain,
The men rejoice in the spoils of blood; victorious again.

Imagine if the stories had been humble and true,
And of those age-old fables, just a few
Told of brave dragons – peaceful and wise
Words spoken true; a halt to their fiery, cruel and callous
demise.

The kindly dragon would not fear the bloodied wrath of man,

It would live in peace alongside them, as all good dragons can.
Banished would be the bloodshed, and an end to gruesome
death.
Forever glorious and magnificently fiery, the dragon's breath.

I am a Drake Enduring

By Marisca Pichette

That changes into darkness
that takes down vines and weaves a web, a mane
to hold my sadness, my defeats in
that stumbles, trips, skins myself
that follows more than leads
that howls and howls when pains are felt
to myself, to my selves
that aches when yawning
that bends and sometimes breaks
that wants to be where dawn touches
lightest, brightest
that tries and tries and tries
to grow.

Slaying Dragons

By Sean E Britten

The children had never taken much notice of the monstrous skull resting on the dining room table. Their sprawling home was full of curiosities. So many paintings covered the walls that in some rooms they lay in piles a dozen deep. Sculptures and other artworks blocked off sections of rooms and hallways. Musical instruments and museum artefacts lay in disorganised heaps like the world's greatest hoarder's nest. Mountains of books, records, CDs and DVDs. The adults called it a 'time capsule'. They were always coming back with more things to add to the stacks.

None of the kids were old enough to remember anything before the mansion. They were let outside only rarely but there were always more of the rooms to explore. Sometimes the adults tried to show them something, like a painting of some dumb soup cans, or some old piece of paper signed by a bunch of stupid names under bulletproof glass, like they were something important. But the kids had grown up surrounded by mysteries of the old world and these things were just parts of the whole. None of them had ever seen a living dog or a cat or anything like that either, so they hadn't worked out that the skull must have belonged to a living thing once until now. To them, it was just another weird sculpture.

"I don't think it's real, I think it's pretend!" Kellie declared, not the oldest but usually the ringleader among the kids through force of personality.

"Teeth!" Three-year-old Abby added.

"My daddy says it's a dinosaur! I told you, it's a dinosaur!" Harrison, a little older than Kellie at six-and-a-half, said.

"I think it's a monster," five-year-old Owen said. "Rawr!"

The families didn't really eat in the dining room. It was big and windowless and used mostly for storing piles and piles of boxes filled with cans of food and dry goods, and stacks of bottled water. The skull dominated the exceptionally long table. As long as a motorcycle, made of whitish-brown, bonelike rock. Teeth as big as knives bristled from its mouth. Gaping eye sockets followed them no matter where they moved. The eight children studied it from different angles, climbing onto the chairs and tabletop.

A door swung open at the far end of the room and the children jumped as if one of the skull's living relatives might have come to visit. Uncle Kevin wandered inside. His face brightened as he saw the kids.

"Hey, what are you rugrats up to?" Uncle Kevin shouted.

"Uncle Kev!" Abby sprinted clumsily across the room and Kevin easily scooped her up in one hand.

Uncle Kev wasn't related to any of the kids, and he and his wife, Grace, didn't have any children of their own. He always found time though to entertain the little ones. A big man with a barrel chest and thick arms, his bushy beard and braided hair made him look like a modern Viking. A couple of pistols and knives were strapped to his body armour and a hatchet dangled from a sheath on his left hip. Kev was careful not to let Abby or any of the kids get too close to the weapons as they swarmed toward him.

"Uncle Kev, where did this thing on the table come from? Is it really a skull?" Kellie asked.

"Oh, that?" Kev glanced casually toward the old bones. "That's a dragon, I slew it."

"No it's not!" Kellie said.

"Yes it is, look at it! It's a dragon skull."

"What's a slew?" Harrison said.

"It means I killed it, in an epic battle."

"Dragons aren't real!" Kellie pressed on.

"They're not real anymore, they used to be."

Uncle Kev ripped open some plastic packaging and pulled a bottle of water from the stack. He walked to the table and settled heavily into one of the chairs. The children massed around him.

"My daddy said it was a-, it was a, teerex," Harrison said. "That's right, a teerex dragon, from the Teerex region," Kev said. "Otherwise it's just a sparkling fire lizard."

Uncle Kev let the appendage at the end of his right arm fall to the table, thumping and gouging the wood. The prosthetic looked something like the end of a fireman's tool, with a hook shaped like a pry bar and an additional spike. It was solid and heavy enough to pound a brick to powder.

"In fact, fighting the dragon was how I lost my right hand," Kev said.

"You told me you lost your hand in a volcano!" Kellie said.

"You remember that?" Uncle Kevin looked surprised.

"You said you lost it fighting Iron Man!" Owen said.

"Iron Man and the Incredible Hulk. But I was just joking about that, that wasn't a real fight! It was a playfight, they were good guys, I wouldn't want to fight them!"

"You said you lost it rescuing a-, a-, a fair maiden." Harrison stumbled over the words as he tried to remember the right phrase.

"That's right! I did, I lost it rescuing a fair maiden from a dragon, from this dragon, in fact!"

Something thundered outside, a loud blast. The shockwave rattled the walls. Most of the children, used to such noises, ignored it completely. Kellie fixed Uncle Kev with a firm stare. Her scepticism often made her look older than her six years. Already, over time, she'd learned to trust that little of what Uncle Kev said had any real relationship with the truth. At the same time his stories were often a good deal more entertaining than what the other adults told them, and Kellie knew what was a higher priority.

"What happened?" Kellie demanded seriously. "No fibbing!"

"With the dragon? Well, this was before, you know, before. Before any of you were born. I was parked at a drive-through waiting to get a breakfast burrito."

"What's a breakfast burrito?" Owen asked.

"Ah, unfortunately another treasure that's been lost to the sands of time. A delicacy you children may never know in this cruel world! I was waiting for my breakfast burrito when a terrible shadow fell across my car and I heard a great, shrieking roar! I looked up and saw a huge, winged serpent flying through the sky above me!"

"They could fly?" Another little girl, Polly, asked.

"Oh, yes, all dragons could fly except for those placed on the No-Fly List. No dragons wanted to mess with the TSA. Even the ones that could fly had to take off their shoes and could carry only teensy little bottles of liquid with them."

"You're fibbing!" Kellie said.

"My hand to Garth." Kev held up his spiked prosthetic. "I had to wait a few minutes before my burrito and my extra-large, half-foam, soy Frappuccino were ready, but as soon as they were, I gave chase!"

A couple of adults passed through the room, Harrison and Polly's mom and dad. Assault rifles dangled off their shoulders. They looked tired but smiled at the kids gathered around Uncle Kev's feet.

"I followed the sounds of chaos, big roars and explosions, and police sirens. Up ahead, I could see buildings on fire and smoke blanketing the sky. The police were trying to fight the dragon! It was huge, with scales like steel and wings as big as a 747!"

"What's that?" Harrison asked.

"Oh, that's a kind of airplane, or it was. Imagine wings, each as long as this room! Its head, well, you can see how big its head was, and its teeth. It had a big, snakelike neck and terrible claws! The police were trying to fight it but they couldn't shoot it, because it was a red dragon and not a black dragon. It wouldn't have mattered anyway, bullets bounced right off its scales because they were so tough."   Kevin poked himself repeatedly in the chest, miming bullets bouncing away. "The dragon breathed gusts of fire that were so hot they set the asphalt and the cars on fire, and its claws pulled apart their cars like tin cans."

"No! Bad!" Abby said.

"I think you're telling lies," Kellie said, and Kev struggled not to break down laughing at her expression.

"Luckily, I had my ancestral sword in the trunk of my car next to the spare. It was hundreds of years old and had magical powers. Only ancestral swords work against dragons. As soon as I'd finished my breakfast, I got out of the car to get it. Unfortunately, during the time it took me the dragon finished what it was doing. See, dragons only like two things, gold, and kidnapping fair maidens. This dragon had come into the city to steal a big vault of gold from the bank. It was carrying the gold away when it spotted a fair maiden in her car. So, it picked up the car in its teeth, and all the gold, and it flew away!"

"And then what happened?" Owen asked.

"I knew someone had to rescue that fair maiden, so I got back in my car and followed the dragon. My car, I just want you to know, was a super cool one, like a Maserati or something. I had to track the dragon for many days but I won't bore you with all the tales of my adventures. Some of them are a bit too PG-13 for all of you, but there were many adventures I'll tell you about some other day. Finally, I tracked the dragon to its lair. In a volcano."

Uncle Kev looked pointedly at Kellie, raising his eyebrows. Little arms crossed over her chest, Kellie didn't look completely sold on his story but her face considered the possibility. Gunfire echoed from outside the mansion. Again none of the kids reacted. Kev looked around and listened, to see if whoever was firing might need help, but when there was only one burst he settled back down.

"With my family's magic sword, I snuck into the dragon's lair. Eventually, I came to a big, rock balcony overlooking a pool of lava, like in Lord of the Rings, which none of you have seen. There were piles and piles of gold and jewels and precious stuff everywhere. I saw the fair maiden tied up to a post near one of the piles of gold. And then I heard a voice say, 'WHAT ARE YOU DOING IN MY HOME, LITTLE HUMAN?'"

"The dragon could talk?" Harrison asked.

"That's right, all dragons can talk. I told him, 'Foul beast, I have come to rescue yon fair maiden from your evil clutches!' Because that's how you've got to talk to dragons, there's a way these things are done. The dragon came out of the cave where it had been hiding. It looked bigger than ever, with flames coming out of its nostrils."

"Then what happened?" Kellie said.

"We fought for hours and hours. I avoided the dragon's claws and teeth and fire, but even with all its magic my sword couldn't cut through its scales! I worked out the only way I could get to him was to stab him in the mouth, where he didn't have any scales. I almost had him, but I wasn't fast enough and his teeth snapped shut on my wrist, biting off my right hand!"

Kev gestured wildly with his hooked prosthetic. Although the children were more than used to it, they reacted as if seeing it for the first time.

"No!" Owen said.

Uncle Kev glanced over at the doorway and saw his wife, Grace, waiting on him. An assault rifle hung off her shoulder. Her expression looked stern as she gestured for him to follow.

"What happened then, Uncle Kev?" Harrison asked.

"Well, kids, I've got to go but to make a long story short, I figured out the only way to get my sword back and to get past the dragon's scales was to trick him into swallowing me! In his stomach, I found my sword and I cut my way out from the inside! Never found my hand though."

The children all expressed amazement and disbelief. They clamoured around him, asking more questions. Knowing Kev struggled to disappoint the kids, Grace hurried over.

"Sorry, guys! Uncle Kev has to come with me, but he can tell you the rest of the story later, okay?"

"Awww," the kids all chimed.

"Your parents told me to tell you to head down to the basement and lock yourselves in! Don't open the door until one of us comes and says the special password. What's that password again?"

"Swordfish," the kids all intoned dutifully.

"That's right, now go!" Grace turned on her husband. "Come on, dragon slayer."

The kids filed away, chattering excitedly, but Kellie stopped Kevin before he could leave. "Uncle Kev?"

"Yeah, honey?"

"What happened to the fair maiden that the dragon kidnapped?"

Kev grinned and jerked his head toward Grace. "What do you think? I married her."

Smiling from ear to ear, Kellie hurried to join the others. Kev followed Grace into the hallway and toward the front of the house, collecting a hulking machine gun along the way. He held it left-handed, his right-hand prosthetic locking on underneath. Grace looked annoyed so he gave her an incorrigibly boyish smile.

"How long were you listening?" Kev asked.

"Long enough," Grace said.

The two of them left via the front doors of the mansion. Dark clouds shadowed the day. The enormous house had been chosen for its defensive position, built on a long spit of land with ocean views and water on three of its four sides. The landward side of the property had been enhanced with trenches and barricades, and snarls of razor wire. More barricades covered the mansion's windows and other entrances. Guns and artillery crowded the front of the house, aimed toward the mainland. A dozen other adults, all armed, waited for them to arrive.

"Kids are in the bunker, what's the sit-rep?" Grace asked.

Jordan, Kellie and Abby's father, answered. "Another wave on the way in. The biggest one yet, they definitely know where we are now and want to wipe us out."

Around them, fifty calibre anti-aircraft guns started thundering. Every fourth round was a tracer, searing orange across the air as they narrowed on the spit passage between them and the mainland. They chewed apart the first ranks of the enemy but there were more coming, many, many more. Their eyes glowed purple in the dusk. Tentacles and insectile limbs bristled from bodies warped and mutated by dark energies. Some towered above the horde like giants. They weren't all once human, some had been animals, and some were so impossibly twisted that it was hard to say what they'd been originally. A few huge, batlike monstrosities whirled above the coming horde. Death meant nothing to them, and those at the front showed no hesitation even as their fellow abominations were chewed to ribbons.

"I don't get it," Grace raised her voice over the weapons, while she still had time to talk. "With everything happening in the world, you've got to make those kids afraid of dragons coming to get them too?"

Kev shouldered his M240 and measured the distance between them and the opening ranks of the horde. Those that had escaped the carnage inflicted by the fifty cals reached the trenches and coils of razor wire.

"It's not about making them afraid of dragons!" Kev said. "It's letting them know that, no matter what the odds, dragons can still be slayed!"

Bloated orange fireballs suddenly consumed a tightly packed section of the horde, as someone triggered several explosive packages buried in shallow graves along the spit of land. The blasts rocked them backward, even standing behind the mansion's barricades, and they felt the heat on their faces. Pieces of the infected launched hundreds of metres into the air and rained back down in the ocean. In overlapping bursts, Kev, Grace, and the other adults began to fire.

Son of a Salamander

By Mark Mills

The dragon crawled with excruciating slowness to the chained maiden. Screaming, crying, thrashing against her iron bonds–there was no escape. The townspeople watched in horror as the sacrificial girl tired, ceasing all struggling, and accepted her fate. The dragon wrapped its snakelike body around the sacrificial stone and turned its scaly head to the townspeople.

"You have done as I commanded. Your village is spared–for now."

Then the dragon opened its impossibly toothy jaws and leaned toward the maiden. The townspeople squeezed their eyes shut until they heard a sickening smack.

They looked to see the dragon nibbling its talons while the girl was still chained to the stone, confused but completely intact.

"If this is your idea of hospitality," the dragon growled, "I am simply appalled. I specifically requested a virgin and this," he waved his tail toward the girl "does not fit the description. If I can't find decent service in these parts, I'll just have to look elsewhere."

And at that the dragon shot through mountains and was gone. The townspeople should be excused the shock that overcame them—this is not typical dragon behavior; in fact, only one in all of history would act in such a manner. This one dragon, Chester Firetail, was in many other ways unlike any other dragon ever born. If truth be told, Chester was not completely a dragon at all.

Chester's mother was a flying dragon, the beautiful kind that soar high overhead with huge wings like rose-colored kites that could transform a mere candle into a sunset of glory. While she was a perfect example of dragon-kind, Chester's father was a mere salamander—no, not the amphibian you might find under stones or in creek beds, but the magical sort that swim in lakes of lava in bubbling volcanoes.

His parents had a fairytale romance but before Chester was six years old, both were unjustly slain by a rampaging knight. Alone in the world, Chester was neither accepted by the dragons nor the salamanders and was forced to live out his childhood in isolation.

Chester stood only five and a half feet tall but was slightly over forty feet long, most of which being his whip-like tail. Although wingless, his short, stout legs could move like the west wind, and, while he could breathe no fire, Chester could run so fast that tracks of flame blazed behind him. Perhaps physically he was less impressive than his flying cousins who could incinerate a town with a single belch but Chester had a cunning and wily mind that made him at least as dangerous.

He really hadn't known if the girl on the stone was a virgin or not; in any case, her reputation would never be the same. As he thought about it, he flipped in somersaults leaving a loop of fire in the air, snorting the laughter of a most satisfied wyrm.

Chester wasn't truly evil, as many dragons are, but thought very little of humans, as all dragons do. As he ran, he found a parson's cottage, tapped on the windows with his tail, and danced an obscene jig on the holy man's porch.

"Well, I never," said the parson's wife as her husband swooned.

Chester laughed with glee and shot up to the mountains, blazing a trail of fire behind him. Once he found a place that was just about right he stopped, wrapped his tail around his body twice, and went to sleep.

***

He awoke late in the night as a very foolish rabbit scampered over his foot. After his snack, Chester saw what had spooked the bunny: a fire a few hundred yards away.

Chester snickered and crept towards the light. He felt long overdue for a bout of mischief.

In this stretch of the hills only an ogre or a troop of goblins would dare flaunt their camp so brazenly. Chester slithered up silently toward it, not because he was scared or respectful of the fire's master but to see what sort of trouble he could pull.

To his surprise he saw, instead of a pack of monsters, the fire was tended by a single old man. The man's head was bare except for seven or eight hairs on his scalp, two or three on his chin, and quite a few on his ears. He looked as wrinkled and fragile as an old leaf and even though Chester was careful not to make a sound, the old man tilted his head toward him and shouted.

"Who's there? Who is it? Answer me."

"Merely a friendly traveler," Chester answered in the dark. "Looking for a bite to eat."

At that Chester snaked his head into the fire light and leered hungrily at the old man.

"Have a bit of cheese," the old man offered. "I've been told that it's green on one side only."

The old man held the cheese out in a direction toward Chester's left and even in the dim light of the fire he could see a thick milky fog covering the old codger's eyes.

"No, thank you," Chester said dejectedly. "I seem to have lost my appetite."

"More for me," the old man replied. "Tell me if I may inquire, can you be described as a stout and strapping fellow?"

"Relatively," Chester answered suspiciously.

"Such is why I'm out here. My village has a problem that you might be able to solve. You're not busy for the next few days, are you?"

A smile returned to Chester's jaws. "Certainly not. It would be a great pleasure to assist you."

The old man smiled and Chester went to sleep again.

The next day as they were approaching the old man's village, Chester decided on his entrance. "I'm a bit shy, you know. You go ahead and announce you've found a hero. Then I'll come up and meet everybody. It's much more of a show that way."

The old man frowned but did as Chester instructed. Chester waited on the far side of a hill and listened as the old man tramped away to meet his friends. If any of them had thought to, they might have spotted Chester's pointy ears sticking over the peak of the hill, but how often does anyone do that in everyday life?

"He said he'd be coming any minute now," Chester heard the old man say and at that he coiled into a spring and bounded into the heart of the village.

There was a great gasping as if a school of large fish suddenly found themselves beached and then a scream. Chester was grinning until his sensitive dragon ears told him that it was not really a scream at all. The blasted fools were cheering.

A brass band began to play and a mob of deranged lunatics slapped Chester on the back and hugged him vigorously. The emotions that flooded Chester's heart were those that only can be found in a practical joker whose prize trick has just horribly backfired. Chester opened his mouth, closed it, and opened it again before a stout man in a top hat strode up to him and offered his hand.

Chester would have much preferred to have slunk under a rock but in his shame lifted his short foreleg which the man pumped. "Glad to have you. Dang glad, if you pardon my Elvish. As the duly appointed representative of the Not Getting Slaughtered Committee, I'd like to present you the key to the village."

Chester dutifully accepted the scrap of tin and, considering he had no pockets to stuff it in, shifted it back and forth in his claws.

"Told you he was shy," said the old man.

"Oh, no need to be nervous," said the man in the top hat who Chester by now identified as the mayor as well as NGS

Committee rep. "At least not here. Mr. Frenton did tell you about our little problem?"

"Er, actually no," Chester managed to croak. "Nothing except you had one."

"We do indeed," said the mayor. "Nothing you can't handle to be sure but something beyond our abilities. You see in the woods north of our village lives the biggest, meanest, and cruelest princess that ever saw the sun. Her name is Georgina."

It's a well-known fact that all dragons are at the very least a little frightened by the name "George." It has been said that some bear such a phobia that they eliminate the letter "G" from their language entirely and speak of how "reen the rass is today." Chester was only half dragon but still shuddered at the fearsome moniker.

"A princess?" Chester repeated.

"A brute of a princess if ever one lived," old Mr. Frenton told him. "Built like a lump of scrap iron eight feet tall and three foot thick. Ever is she abusing our village, insulting our physical appearance, punching, pinching—oh, it must end. It must end."

"Mind you," the mayor assured him, "she is a princess subject to insomnia if a pea slips under her mattress and as far as we can tell a virgin."

Although he said it to cheer Chester and soften Frenton's words, the mayor actually disturbed him even further. Chester's father had always told him that a dragon that steered clear of royalty, particularly virtuous royalty, would live for a ripe old age. Avoiding royalty named after *He Who Bore the Lance* went without saying.

"Why, of course I'll do it," Chester agreed. "Which direction is she?"

As one the townspeople swung a finger to the south.

"Before you begin your quest, you need to know the most essential—"

"No time for that," Chester blurted and tore off southward. Once he was out of sight, he swerved to the east and ran nonstop for eighteen miles.

When he stopped, it wasn't because of weariness but guilt. He knew that even the slightest practical joke could hurt and whatever Georgina was to the townspeople, it certainly was more than a joke. If they'd been willing to send an old man in the wilderness to search for salvation, the least he could do was investigate. If nothing else, such as a hideous individual might give him a few ideas for new jokes. He reckoned the direction of her castle and took off to it.

The castle was a glum place full of bones and spikes with skulls on them, the type of place only architects with rampant psychosis might design. A wall breached only by thick doors of steel stood around the fortress. There didn't seem to be any noise behind it. He ran right up the side of the wall, leaving a trail of ashes upon it. He could see nothing; he could smell nothing, and the lack of anything big and scary helped his confidence immensely. He began to bang his challenge against the door of the castle.

Georgina was just in the middle of breakfast and burst from her kitchen frothing at the mouth, spewing out bits of kidney pie and rancid tea. In the meanwhile, Chester had reached into his bag of tricks and selected what he liked to call the "Ghost

Dragon." Essentially it was a pale forty-foot potato sack that Chester slipped into to give the effect of an undead dragon. It was fairly unelaborate, working mainly on sheer size, and unfortunately, size was an element failed to impress Georgina.

"Boo!" Chester wailed at her approach. "I am the ghost of Christmas—"

Chester never got a chance to finish. Without ceremony, Georgina belted him in the snout, knocking him in a bundle in the end of the potato sack. She then grabbed the sack by the other end, swung it around her head three times, and flung it halfway to the sea.

"My goodness," Chester exclaimed when he finally unraveled himself. "A sourpuss of the upmost level. Perhaps something a tad more subtle is in order."

He tried disguising his tail as a traveling salesman and using it as a puppet but before he was able to begin his sales pitch, Georgina had heaved an axe at him forcing him to flee to the forest.

He thought of soaping her windows, of hot foots, and whoopee cushions. He thought of all sorts of things before he realized, perhaps a dragon could stand up to somebody named George (or at least a derivative).

***

Chester's shenanigans put Georgina in a particularly bad mood that morning. Although she would never admit it to anyone, all her mornings were pretty bad. Georgina had once presided over a royal court and a small army of servants but all had fled before her grouchiness. She was grumbling over the mess she'd left in the kitchen when she heard a banging against her door. That stupid knocker again!

She grabbed her sword and snatched up her shield and stomped to the door and flung it open to find nobody there.

At first, she wondered if she might have imagined it but then her bad mood caught up with her. She bellowed into the woods, swearing so fiercely that it shook leaves off the trees. She turned her back and slammed the door behind her.

She knew there was something tremendously annoying in the area but she didn't know what. There'd been something odd in that potato sack and that odd puppet disguised as a human, but Georgina couldn't decide what exactly that something was. She certainly couldn't figure why, with her reputation, it would act so outlandishly.

Before she had taken thirty steps, the knocking began again. Georgina rushed back to the door and flung it open again. This time there was the scent of burnt leaves in the air but nothing else. She shut the door again and waited.

When the joker knocked his first time, she kicked open the door to find her welcome mat afire. She stomped it out with her combat boots and then began to scream.

***

Most dragons, even the really evil ones, bury their dung so deep that only the trolls and goblins are bothered by it. Due to their fiery nature, dragon droppings make cow pies smell like roses and dead fish seem fresh.

Georgina had just discovered a huge amount of it caked onto her brand-new boots. Like an earthbound comet, Georgina strode toward the village, steam puffing out her ears. They were the only ones nearby. They had to be behind this insanity.

Even in her anger, as she walked, she began to notice something peculiar. Farther off down the path came a billowing of smoke accompanied by the scent of burning wood and hair. Before she could put anything together, she glanced up to the branches above her and froze.

Chester slithered down the bough of an old oak and wound himself in a coil a few feet in front of Georgina. "Good morning Princess," he said. "You seem to be in a hurry."

"Why, yes I was," Georgina despite her rage was more than a little put off by seeing a dragon poised above her. Despite her magic sword and shield, she felt uneasy. "I was just on my way to the village. If you don't mind me, I'll be on my way."

"You needn't bother." Chester swung out his tail to block her way. "You see I've just eaten the village."

Georgina's unease yielded to trembling. "You mean you've eaten all the people?"

"All the people, all the cattle, all the dogs, all the houses, even all the bricks from the church. But you know, I'm in the mind for dessert."

Even Georgina with her magic weapons would have needed some sort of strategy to take out the entire town and the thought of someone eating church bricks made her knees wobble. As a child, her father had terrified her with tales of a stone-eating ogre that lived under her bed and she had often wet her sheets rather than risk scurrying to the chamber pot at night.

"Err, I've never really cared for masonry if truth be told," she stammered. She wanted desperately to be home in her castle but didn't dare turn her back on the dragon. "I imagine it's good for one's nails."

"Hmmm," Chester ignored her words but snaked his neck behind her. "I was wondering what to have as afters. Thank goodness you came along."

Georgina jumped forward just as Chester's teeth snapped shut behind her backside. She dropped her sword, dropped her shield, and, without thought took off running forward, towards the village. Chester could have easily caught her but she had no way of knowing it.

It wasn't until she ran into the village and shimmied up the flagpole that she realized she had been had. But by then it was too late: she was defenseless with a mob of townspeople armed with rotten apples and old sausage and she couldn't get down until somebody brought a ladder.

I'm sorry to say that Georgina never really gave up her bullying. But without her magic sword and shield, she could never achieve the threat that she once was. She blustered local merchants and never waited in lines but eventually fit into life in the village, never again tempting the townspeople to scout for heroes to put her in her place. Eventually in her later years she did mellow to the point that she allowed the castle to be used as a theater at Christmas time.

Chester became the local hero and mascot. Despite a small misgiving at first, he settled in a local cave and attracted a lady dragon who found his lack of wings not so disturbing. Even after seven centuries the town still remembered him with a rugby team known as the Salamanders. Yet, even after chasing Georgina up the flagpole, Chester never gave up his mischievous ways.

"We can't thank you enough," the mayor told him. "Could we get you anything to make up for your troubles?"

"Well stop me if you heard this one before," Chester replied with a smile. "But have you got any virgins?"

Tumble Dry, Low

By Andrew Murphy

This was the fifth time in as many months.

It was honestly getting out of hand.

Scott had always heard his mother pitch a veritable fit about socks going missing whenever she'd done the washing, but he'd never paid it any mind. At the time, such things hadn't seemed to matter all that much, especially seeing as he wasn't the one buying the socks.

Now that he was? Well, it was a tad bit more annoying.

Thing was, Scott knew he wasn't alone. Everyone lost a sock or two in the dryer, and yet not a single soul seemed all that certain where they wound up.

Oh, he'd heard the stories, the theories. That they fell apart in the cycle and turned into the bits of lint that filled up the trap. Or that someone or another had taken their dryer apart piece by piece and discovered a whole collection which had someone made their way deep into the machine.

He very much doubted the veracity of the former and lacked the skills to even attempt the latter. Thus, Scott tried his best to ignore it.

But we all have our limits. His being five socks in as many months.

One or two mix-and-matched pairs he could handle, but all

those lone socks whose twins were lost somewhere within the bowels of the dryer were far too much. Something had to be done.

Scott just didn't have the slighted idea what that something was.

Were he more technically inclined, perhaps he would put a small GPS device on a pair and toss them inside so he could track where they wound up.

Lacking such things, however, he decided on something far more low-tech.

Bringing along a fresh load, he threw it inside and started up the dryer as he had countless times before. Only this time, he had a plan.

Sort of.

This time, when it was around halfway through its cycle, Scott tore the door open and stuck his head inside as far as he could.

What awaited him there was not what he had expected. Not in the slightest.

His clothes were there, of course, scattered across the drum of the dryer as they should be. But they were not alone.

Sitting there in a small crevice that Scott had never noticed before, was what could only be described as a rather small dragon.

Scott knew for a fact that it was a dragon, rather than some wild lizard that had somehow wandered inside and decided to make a home for itself in the dryer, due to several factors.

The first one being that he lived in a northern climate that had a severe lack of wild lizards, at least as far as he knew.

The second one being the creature had a pair of wings sprouting out from its back that he knew no lizards were currently in possession of, useful as they might be evolutionary-speaking.

And the last, as well as the most important one, was that the creature looked exactly how one would picture a dragon, if only on the slightly smaller side of things.

Staring at the unexpected sight before him, it took Scott several moments longer than perhaps it should have for him to notice that said dragon was resting comfortably on a small pile of fabric. A pile which, upon further observation, was clearly made up of all his missing socks. Not simply the ones he had lost recently, but some which had been missing for months. All of them piled up beneath the dragon.

The dragon who, such as it was, had seemed to notice him.

"This hoard belongs to me," it said in a soft yet powerful voice, tiny limbs and small but still sharp claws stretching out over the sock pile protectively.

"I beg to disagree," Scott began, still somewhat taken aback by the sheer fact that there was a dragon in his dryer, let alone one whom he was now conversing with. "Those are my socks."

Looking down at the pile upon which it rested, then back at Scott, the dragon shook its scale-covered head. "These offerings were sent to me and me alone. Thus, they are mine."

Considering this for a moment, Scott had to admit that he understood where the dragon was coming from, at least to some degree. Were he in its position, it would certainly seem that randomly appearing pieces of clothing could be constituted as offerings, even if they clearly were not. Regardless, he hoped that common sense would overcome such a thing, or at least as much as possible given the otherwise absurd situation at hand.

"I was unaware anyone was currently residing inside this dryer. Had I known, I'd never have started putting any 'offerings', as you call them, inside."

From where he knelt, half-crouched with his head inside the machine, Scott watched the dragon's eyes widen and its jaw open as a small laugh escaped it. The laugh quickly grew into a larger one, and within seconds the dragon was on its scaly backside, its body racked by utter hysterics.

Scott did not see what was so funny, but as its giggles subsided, the dragon seemed more than willing to elaborate. "Unaware? Unaware? How did you think the rest of these things got dry? Magic?"

Although he knew in his heart there was another reason- one more scientifically based and having something to do with heat and air and other such things, Scott was unsure. As with a great many appliances and bits of technology one uses in their day-to-day life, he wasn't one-hundred percent certain that he truly understood how any of them truly worked. After all, like so many of us, he had never looked into how this thing or that did whatever it does. He simply accepted that they did whatever they were supposed to, paid his bills, and went on with his life. It all had to make sense, didn't it?

He wasn't so sure anymore.

"Um... Well... I never gave it all that much thought."

The dragon huffed, and its expression clearly showed its disdain. "Well, that's your fault then, isn't it? Comfy trinkets like these are the price you pay for dry clothes. Don't like it, hang 'em outside."

As logical a proposition as that might have appeared to some, Scott had neither the time nor the space to hang his clothes out long enough to get them sufficiently dry. It's why he'd bought a dryer in the first place.

Which left him only one course of action.

"Fine," he sighed as he shut the dryer door, accepting the likely loss of countless more socks in his future.
Scott stared at the machine for several moments after he turned it back on. And his mind began to wander and wonder about what other sorts of strange creatures were possibly hiding in the various appliances around his otherwise humble home.

He quickly decided he was better off not knowing.

After all, a tiny dragon in ones dryer was one thing. A baby Kraken swimming somewhere in the bowels of the washing machine or an abominable snowman hiding out deep within the freezer would be something else entirely.

Besides, they might expect something far greater than simple socks.

And socks were certainly a small price to pay for peace of mind.

Orange to Blue

By Jessica Turnbull

Water whizzes past my head, twirling in the air. The black dragon beside me gives chase to it, his tail wagging like a dog's. He is just over six feet tall, but when he flares his wings out it makes him look so much bigger. Once he manages to chomp on the water, it falls to the floor as if it never moved. He looks back at me with his sparkling turquoise eyes, sticking his tongue out as a sign for me to do it again.

"One last time, Aqueous." I tell him. "But then we need to get ready for the festival."

I flick my fingers and a bubble of water appears in front of my palm. He lowers himself to the floor and tucks his wings behind him as it starts to float towards him. I can see that it's taking every inch of his will not to spring forward before it gets close enough. When the bubble is in reach he springs, but I twirl my wrist and it darts to the side. My companion whines and gives me a glare before giving chase. Once he reaches the edge of the forest however, I know it's time to stop. The bubble pops, but Aqueous doesn't move. His snout is slightly raised, and his nostrils are flaring.

Before I can even open my mouth, he's darted into the trees. The thick green leaves quickly swallow his body, and if it weren't for the trail of broken twigs behind him, I never could have followed him.

"Aqueous! This isn't funny!"

There's a yelp from ahead and my heart sinks. What if he's hurt? What if he went after something too big? What if one of the guards found him?

I deliberately push those thoughts to the back of my mind and run after him. The air instantly chills when I step inside, and although I was roasting before, I miss the warm sun beaming down on my back. I follow Aqueous' small path of destruction, suddenly grateful for his clumsiness and inability to keep quiet. My foot catches on a root and I reach out towards a nearby tree to steady myself. When my hand touches the rough bark, it also touches something wet and sticky. I quickly pull away, inspecting the fresh crimson on my fingers. It has a metallic smell, and my heart sinks.

"Aqueous, come back! Right now, I mean it!"
There are more panicked yaps from ahead and my legs move of their own accord. Horrible thoughts of my companion attacked, possibly dying, fills my head. I *can't* lose him.

Finally, I spot something black moving in the trees in front of me. He's halfway up a tree, his claws digging into the bark. His tail is lashing, and his lips are pulled back in a snarl.
"There you are!" I pant, allowing my beating heart to slow. "I found blood and I thought-"

He retreats from the tree, sticking his rump out to steady himself. He continues pointing up into the tree with his paw, yapping about whatever is up there. After glaring at him for a few moments to let him know that he shouldn't have run off, I

follow his gaze. At first it looks normal. The leaves are thick
and full, obscuring most of the branches underneath. Then
something shifts behind them. Gingerly I move closer to the
tree, spotting more patches of blood along the trunk. I squint
to see through the foliage, and the shape moves again.

Aqueous yanks me back as a dragon head emerges from the
leaves. Unlike Aqueous, whose head is broader and blockier,
this one is thin, with sharp features. Its scales are a pale orange,
but around the eyes they are dotted with flecks of black. The
more it stretches towards us, I can see more of its neck. It's
covered with orange feathers, most looking dry and ill. The
dragon continues to stretch towards us, its mouth opening in a
hiss.

Amphiptere.

We had learned about them briefly when going over dragon
species in school. They're pack dragons and are rarely seen near
human settlements. They prefer to live in mountains, where
the air is thin, and the temperatures are lower.

Aqueous growls and moves in front of me as the dragon
winds down the tree. Unlike Westerns, like Aqueous, they
have no legs. It has two large wings which are folded over most
of its body. The wing membrane is connected to its body,
stretching across its skin.

Although I feel sorry for it, I can't help but feel relief that
Aqueous isn't hurt. My companion hooks my belt with his claw
and forces me behind him, flaring his wings at the strange
dragon. It pays no attention until it reaches the ground, where
it also flares its wings and hisses. Its easily twice the length of
my companion, and its wings are a lot thinner, but with

hooked horns on top. My companion sinks into a fighting stance, splaying his legs and digging his claws into the dirt. The dragon doesn't look fazed, until water starts dropping out of his mouth. If Aqueous is using our shared element, water, then that can't be a good sign. The dragon squawks and slithers back towards the tree, its yellow eyes narrowed.

"Has it said why it's here?" I ask him.

My companion nods, and I wish that I could speak dragon. It would make communication so much easier.
The dragon shifts its gaze from me to Aqueous and unfurls itself from the tree. The dragon shifts forward, and Aqueous hisses, spitting a few globs of water at it.
I back off a few steps, not taking my eyes off it. "We should go, before the guards find us."

I haven't seen any of the guard dragons too much, but I know that they patrol every wall of the camp that we live in. They don't want anything getting out, or in. The sight of dragons in bulky golden armour used to scare me, but now I'm used to it. Luckily for me, Aqueous isn't feeling argumentative about this situation. We both creep back the way we came, our eyes on the dragon. It doesn't follow us, and instead when we're a considerable distance away it slithers back up the tree it was hiding in.

***

"And you're sure it was an Amphiptere?" Marco asks, brushing his long fringe out of his eyes.

"Yes, I'm sure. I recognised it from my classes. You know that I know my dragons."

Soon after Aqueous and I left the dragon, I went to find one of my friends. I'm not confident enough to deal with this thing on my own. I don't know whether to report it or protect it. I had bumped into Marco and his dragon, Drea, carrying decorations for the festival.

"What exactly do you want to do, Haze?

"I don't know," My eyes shift to my feet. "I should probably turn it in, but then what would happen to it?"

"I dunno, they'll probably sell it as an exotic pet."

"Not funny."

Aqueous and Drea start conversing in low growls, the two of them nod their heads once.

"What is it, Drea?" Marco asks, patting his companion's neck. "You know something we don't?"

She nods her head and then gestures with her tail towards Aqueous.

"Did it want to hurt me?" I ask him.

He nods his head once, his usually bright eyes steely.

"Do you want to help it though?"

He looks towards Drea, who just shrugs at him. His ears flatten and he lets out a playful growl. The white dragon just flicks her tail in response. He then looks at me and nods once more.

"Another adventure, huh?" Marco elbows my side. "We haven't done one of those in a while."

"Because the last one gave me a massive scar," I remind him, brushing my hair over my face. The pink line stretches across my left eyebrow towards my nose. Over the years, it has faded but it's still noticeable.

He tucks my hair behind my ear again. "There's nothing wrong with a battle scar," He looks into my eyes for a moment before looking away. "Show us where this thing is then."

I point to the discarded box of plastic yellow and black flags. "What about the festival?"

"Pfft," He rolls his eyes, kicks the box, and says sarcastically: "I don't care about that. This sounds much more fun."

"Fine, but don't blame me if you get in trouble."
He makes a cross gesture over his heart and winks. I roll my eyes before looking around to make sure no-one has noticed us talking. The square is mostly empty, apart from the occasional person or dragon putting up decorations or setting up food stalls. A lot of artwork, made of painted dragon pawprints, has already started to be nailed to the buildings around it. The Fire and Dark Elementals love these festivals, but it doesn't make much difference to everyone else. As a Water Elemental, I don't mind too much, but having some nice food and spending time with my friends doesn't sound too bad.

Marco nudges my arm. "Come on, if we hurry, we can get back before they set up the doughnut stall."
I can already feel my mouth watering. "There's a doughnut stall?"

We jog down the empty streets, and for once I'm glad that hardly anyone is around. A few plastic flags and balloons have been strung up across the wooden cabins, each fluttering in different colours. It's nice to have a chance not to worry about school and dragon training for once. Aqueous and I have a great bond, but our Elemental power needs work.

Once we get close to the field where Aqueous and I were supposed to be practicing, my nerve starts to falter. This dragon isn't against doing Marco and I harm, should I really bring him along?

"Maybe you and Drea should go back." I blurt out, just loud enough for him to hear.

"No way! We're part of this now. Come on, I've got Drea to protect me." He pats his companion on the snout, who just snorts in response. "We'll be fine."

Still not convinced, Drea takes the lead, and he follows her with a grin. Aqueous noses my back to get me moving again too.

"Where did Aqueous find it?" Marco asks.
I don't need to answer, as Drea is already tasting the air and moving towards the spot Aqueous disappeared into. The black dragon follows her with a spring in his step, yapping to her as she tries to concentrate.

"We just need to follow them." I reply with a shrug.
He shakes his head. "There's no need to be a smartass all the time, Drea."
The white dragon rolls her pink eyes and continues to move forward, her nostrils flaring. Aqueous goes to push in front of her, but she whips around and nips his hide. He jumps back with a whimper, bowing his head. His ears prick slightly, and he straightens up. Marco and Drea are a bit ahead, but it takes no time to catch up. Drea keeps the club of her tail at Marco's hip, just in case she needs to move him quickly. Aqueous

copies her, though his tail drops below my knees after a few seconds.

You'll trip me before you can do anything else.

"How much further, Haze?" Marco calls from ahead.

"Not very. We didn't go far."

A glimmer of movement in the tree above him catches my eye. Before I can even open my mouth, a pale orange head darts towards him. Drea's reflexes are quick, and she's able to push him into a nearby bush. The dragon's teeth instead sink into Drea's side, though they don't puncture anything beyond her scales. The white dragon lets out a roar and clamps her front feet around its head and hisses in its face. Aqueous rushes forward, ducking to avoid her clubbed tail as it collides with the dragon's side. A garbled roar erupts from its mouth as my companion bites on its neck, ripping away a few feathers in the process. Its body starts to slink down the trunk, but Marco is still tangled in the bush underneath.

Water blasts out of my palms before it can get any closer to him. The stream smacks the creature's side, drenching some of its feathers. The attack was a weak and desperate one, but it irritates it enough to slide back into the trees.

"Fuck's sake!" Marco grunts, gripping the bush with both his hands. The whole thing instantly erupts into a bright orange flame, making the dragon screech from the branches. "Stupid bushes!"

With her companion safe, Drea's attention is on the Amphiptere. She clambers up the tree in a flash, though due to her muscled frame she can't reach the dragon woven amongst the thick leaves. A purple beam erupts from her mouth and the dragon screams, its bottom half dangling from the tree. Aqueous grabs the tip of its tail and uses all his strength to prevent it from righting itself. Drea continues to swat at it from the front, leaving it trapped with nowhere to go. It then lets out a bleating noise, and all three of them stop. I look at my companion, but his gaze is fixed on the dragon.

What is it saying to you?

After a few moments he lets the dragon's tail go. Drea also retreats down the tree, though her lips are still pulled back in a snarl.

"What's happened?" Marco demands as the creature drops from the tree, though stays near the trunk. "Has it agreed to stop attacking us?"

Now that it is no longer in the tree, I can see its entire body more clearly. Its face is covered in bleeding scratches thanks to Drea, and a few clumps of feathers have been ripped out of its body. The scales underneath are a sickly orange, and some look like they're crumbling or peeling. It looks sick, and I'm worried it might pass on whatever it has to our dragons.

Aqueous and Drea start growling to each other, and I can't help but notice the glare the dragon gives them. Marco stumbles back, pulling charred twigs out of his jacket.

"Are you okay, Haze?"

"Yeah, I'm fine. More worried about you."

A sly smile appears on his face. "It'll take more than a prickly bush to take me down."

Aqueous growls to get our attention. He then points to him and Drea with his tail and the Amphiptere.

"You want to help it?" Marco asks.

Aqueous then points at Marco and I, and then back to Drea.

"Looks like we're involved too." I reply with a smile.

"It's always us, isn't it?"

"I don't know what you mean." I wriggle my eyebrows. "All of our adventures were your idea, after all."

He crosses his arms and raises an eyebrow. "There's a difference between exploring an abandoned tree house and helping an angry dragon." He looks at it, and it responds with a hiss.

"Well, I'm helping it."

His eyes roll so hard that I can only see the whites. "I knew you'd say that."

Aqueous barks something at the dragon. If it had ears, I'm sure they would be permanently pinned to its head with how angry it looks. A single incisor is stuck out over its bottom lip, giving it a permanently unimpressed expression.

"Ugh, fine!" My friend finally relents, uncrossing his arms. "What do we have to do?"

Aqueous and Drea suddenly freeze, their ears perked. They then start snapping at each other, trying to push the dragon forward. I look over my shoulder and notice the faint glint of golden armour.

The guards are coming.

"Go!" I hiss at them. "Take it to one of our cabins if you can."

"What? No way they're going to be able to sneak that thing around!"

With a quick pinch of his arm, he stops complaining and notices the two guards heading towards us. Both dragons are easily eight feet tall, and their large horns make them seem even taller. Their backs, heads and stomachs are covered in plates of gold coloured armour. The design is simple, only meant to give them protection from any kids or dragons who try to escape from camp. There's no point in making them intricate and beautiful if they're just going to scuff it up anyway.

I grab Marco's hand, shooting him a sly smile. "We just snuck away, okay? Nothing out of the ordinary."

"Except for the dragon smell."

My heart sinks. I'd forgotten that their noses are a lot better than ours.

One of the dragons, orange with red stripes, growls at the two of us, its nostrils flaring.

Marco holds our entwined hands up. "Sorry, we didn't realise we had gone so far."

The other dragon, pure emerald green, opens its mouth to taste the air. Its eyes widen and I know it has the smell of the dragon.

"Is… Is something wrong?" I ask, trying to sound innocent but just coming off as nervous. "We can go back."

The green dragon nods sharply and swings its head towards the other, its teeth bared. Just when I think we've been caught, the two dragons stomp around us and further into the trees, their tails swishing.

Once they're out of earshot, Marco mutters: "That was close."

"Let's get out of here before they come back."

After a few steps I realise that we're still holding hands and I untangle my fingers. He looks away, his face going slightly pink.

Just when I think we've gotten away with it, there's a roar. A column of fire is shot into the air, followed by a column of ice soon after it. Our companions come bounding towards us through the trees, their eyes wide.

That can only mean one thing.

They found it.

***

More armoured dragons start arriving just as the sun disappears halfway over the horizon. With celebrations starting soon, we need to find another way to help the Amphiptere. Everyone has been pushed back into the streets and armoured dragons are now patrolling the forest. One man catches my eye, someone who I presume is a family member. The armoured dragons allow him to pass without so much as a sniff.

Who are you?

"Marco." I go to nudge my friend but all I get is empty air.

He and Drea have moved further down the street, a poor attempt at trying not to look suspicious.

His eyes meet mine when I move towards him. "I know that look." He groans.

"They've just let someone through the trees."

"Maybe he's one of the guard's companions."

"Or maybe he already knew the Amphiptere was here. We need to get a closer look."

"And how do you expect us to do that?"

I glance up at the sky, which is now turning pink. Shadows are starting to stretch across the streets, and a chill is in on the breeze. "You're have dark powers as well as fire. You can hide in the shadows."

It's almost as if he's just remembered his second element. It's a rare occurrence to be born with two, but he was one of the lucky ones. "If there are any other Dark Elementals there, they'll see me." Drea taps his shoulder with her tail, giving him a stern look. "Okay, Drea is saying we won't get seen. I get it." He stretches his arms above his head. "Ugh, fine. But try not to get into any trouble before we get back okay?"

"No promises."

His expression is one of fake disappointment before he and Drea sneak behind one of the buildings, where a large shadow has started to form. The armoured dragons then drag something shrouded in blankets past the crowd. Though I can't see it clearly, I'm sure that there are a few orange feathers being left on the ground behind it.

"Excuse me, everyone! Can I have your attention for a few moments?"

The man that walked through the guards earlier is now stood on top of a small wooden crate in the middle of the square.

Once enough people have his attention, his clasps his hands together with a grin. "This is a special night indeed, people and dragons. The summer solstice only comes once a year, and it's time for everyone to celebrate." He continues speaking, despite the confused murmurs of the crowd. "That is why you are in for a special treat tonight.   I have gotten permission from the Head Instructor put on a special... Display for you."

I have a bad feeling about what he's going to say next. Aqueous shifts beside me, his front feet kneading the ground anxiously.

"You may be wondering why we have a built a stage this year." He gestures behind him.

It's made of simple wood, like the other stalls, but is much bigger. A few blue curtains have been strung up around it, as if there will be a big reveal later. There are still people working on it though, so construction isn't finished.

"We have managed to find the dragon that represents the solstice itself. An *Amphiptere*. And I must say, you are in for a delightful surprise."

The crowd starts to murmur excitedly, and a few dragons start wagging their tails.

A hand grabs my shoulder, making me jump until I recognise Marco's voice. "Haze!"

"You scared me!"

"I'm guessing you've heard what they're planning on doing with it."

I look up towards the man, who has a massive grin on his face. "Some sort of display?"

"They're forcing it to do something it isn't ready for; I overheard the guards saying so." He looks around and lowers his voice. "They're worried that it will die before it gets a chance to perform."

The poor thing looked deathly ill the few times I've seen it. Maybe it's the stress of being handled or being around so many people. Either way, it shouldn't be here.

"Don't worry everyone!" The man exclaims above the chatter. "You won't have to wait much longer. Once the sun fully sets, the display can begin."

Behind us, the sun is barely peeking over the horizon now. Whatever we need to do, we need to do it now.

"We need to go, now." I mutter to him.

Marco nods his head, and we detach from the crowd. People are starting to gather around the stage, chatting excitedly about what is about to happen. Drea skirts around them, towards the stage. Bright lights are being put up now, and various pieces of sound equipment are being passed around.

"Did you know, people and dragons," The man continues. "That tonight you will leave not only with a treat memory, but also a souvenir from the Amphiptere? Would you like a beautiful scale? Or possibly a feather? I am willing to help you with that."

The thought sends a shiver down my spine. They're treating a dragon like it's some sort of toy, rather than a living creature. Aqueous shields us with one his dark wings as we duck between the shadows. Drea pops in and out of my vision, her hiding in the shadows tricking my eyes. We make our way to the back of the stage, which is mysteriously bare. Except for a metal cage, far too small to keep the Amphiptere in. Still, the orange dragon has been squished inside, its face pressed against the metal mesh around it. Its eyes are downcast, and half closed, like it's already given up.

We're going to help you, I promise.

Its irises widen slightly when Aqueous starts to creep towards it. Too late, I notice the dragon crouched behind the cage. It jumps at my companion, its red body crushing him from above. Aqueous' mouth opens but only a heavy puff of air comes out. Drea rushes forward with a snarl and tackles the dragon, pinning it to the dirt. Her paw slams on its snout, preventing it from crying out.

From just around the corner, I can see that the sun has completely disappeared over the hills. The sky has already started to darken, while the last rays of sunlight reach the ground. The mesh is cold on my palms and I look for a lock or something that would free it. The dragon starts to shift, and orange scales start to peel from its skin.

My heart pounds even faster. "Something is wrong." Marco pulls a few dried scales out from the mesh. "I don't know if we can save it."

"We can!"

The dragon that Drea has pinned suddenly rears up, bucking her off. A rock is clenched between its teeth, which is then spat at her. With its attention on Drea, Aqueous snaps his jaws on its tail. Before it has the chance to scream, Drea smacks its snout with her tail. The club makes a sickening crack when it connects with its head. The dragon drops to the floor, its tongue lolling out of its mouth.

I'm unable to look any longer as the Amphiptere suddenly writes in its cage. It looks like the entirety of its skin is coming off at once.

"I've got the latch!" Marco hisses and flicks a piece of metal fixed to the floor.

The cage instantly breaks apart, the combined writhing of the dragon inside and poor craftsmanship being its downfall. There are voices from the stage and I'm conflicted. Before I can decide whether to stay, Marco grabs my hand and yanks us back to the hiding place. We crouch behind a pair of empty bins, the foul smell making my nose wrinkle. Drea and Aqueous quickly follow us, flapping their wings as they go.

The man from earlier steps out from the stage, his eyes bugging out of his head. "What happened? How did it get *out*?"

The stage workers are unable to reply when the Amphiptere's body wrenches with a groan. The skin around its head starts to split, and the orange scales start to peel. Its wet head pushes through the dead skin, and it starts to wrench its entire body through. The strange dragon doesn't look like it's in any pain when its orange feathers start to fall out. Its skin starts to rip and tear further as it slithers out, like a snake shedding its skin. Underneath the pale orange scales are brilliant midnight blue ones. Blue feathers pop out of the dead skin, shinier and healthier than the ones getting shed.

"It's shedding." I breathe. "It wasn't sick, it just wanted to shed."

Marco grins and squeezes my hand. "It's amazing."

With most of the Amphiptere escaping from its skin, it starts to snap at the workers around it. None are brave enough to approach to collect any of the pieces that fall of it.

"I want the blue scales too!" The man fumes, running his hand through his hair. "Where are the scissors? Get in there and get them now!"

The thought of them prying the new, healthy scales from its body makes me sick. The Amphiptere clearly isn't too impressed with this either, as it starts hissing at anyone who gets too close to it. Its wings are still too sticky from malting to fly, but it's able to swing its body around to snap at anyone who gets too close. Just a few more seconds, and the sticky liquid will solidify, and it can get away.

A chilly breeze makes me shiver as the dragon sheds the last of its skin. It hooks it with its tail and flings it towards the man and the workers, who don't get the chance to move out of the way in time. Heavy dead scales collide with their chests, and they lose their balance, tumbling in a messy heap. The Amphiptere shakes it head and stretches its wings. Underneath they are completely covered by a sea of dark blue feathers. It flaps twice and starts to lift off the ground. Its yellow eyes meet mine and for a moment I think I see gratitude in them. With a roar, it swoops over us, looking like a flying snake.

Aqueous bounces and waves at the dragon with his tail, while Drea just gives it a cold nod. After circling us once, it takes off into the darkening clouds. Its dark scales soon blend with the blues of the sky and I lose sight of it.
Marco pulls me away from our hiding place. "Quick!"

The workers are starting to shift the shed skin off them. I can also see the dragon that Drea hit earlier starting to stir. We take off, hand in hand, back out into the square. So many people are still gathered around the stage that they don't notice our running entrance. A lot of them are pointing in the direction the Amphiptere flew off in, muttering amongst themselves. Marco let's go of my hand and disappears into the crowd, just as people start to notice what's happening backstage. A minute later, something warm is pushed into my hand and I jump.

"Sorry, didn't mean to scare you," Marco mumbles, his mouth full of fresh doughnut. "We needed a cover story."

The sweet smell of the doughnut makes my mouth water. "A cover story?"

He takes another bite and winks. "You know, just in case."

"You really think two teenagers are going to be the prime suspects of this case?"

"You want the doughnut or not?"

Aqueous' turquoise eyes glitter as he stares up at the sky. He then yaps and noses something silky into my hand. A blue feather, the colour of the midnight sky, almost twice the size of my palm. I twirl it in my fingers and smile.

Summoner of the Jade Dragons

By Linda M Crate

Umma felt her ire rise with each passing word coming out of his mouth. This wanker really considered himself to be a hero? She had seen the way he had spoken to women he fancied. How violent and angry he became when they told him no, and how he slut shamed them afterwards as if he hadn't been the one that had shown interest in them to begin with.

"I'm a nice guy."

"Which says nothing. Nice is fake, nice is a façade, nice is a good descriptor for absolutely nothing," Umma said, shrugging. "Compassion, kindness, sensitivity, and emotional intelligence are the things that truly matter. Nice isn't always nice, and I have found that those that have to announce they're nice often aren't," Umma insisted.

"I'm a nice guy," he insisted, with gritted teeth.

Umma snorted at his response. Unoriginal and not even well developed. Still, one could hope for better. Judging from the violent and angry look upon his face, however, he was incapable of processing things other than the things he would like to hear. Pity for him that Umma was always a woman who had embraced her inner magic and power, and the blacksmith wasn't about to spare him from the hotter side of her tongue.

Umma had heard enough come from Dystorian's mouth to last her a lifetime. If he said he was a nice guy one more time, she had half a mind to sew his mouth shut. She had never been as good at mending and making clothes as her sister Joan, but she made do. She could manage that much, she knew that.

All of her life Umma had to step carefully around Dystorian's and she had enough of it. Why should she and other women have to live in fear of men who refused to accept no as a full sentence let alone an answer? She was exhausted of always having to be polite and contrite, and laughing in uncomfortable situations simply to see that she'd get out of situations alive.

Suddenly, Dystorian was pulling on her custom jade hair pins that were the last gifts her grandmother had given her before, and she gave him a dark look.

"What's with these weird looking hair pins, anyway? It doesn't even resemble a dragon," Dystorian scoffed.

"Dragons take many forms," Umma snapped, fighting to keep her voice even.

"What's the matter, Umma?" Dystorian asked. "I was only curious about your hair pins, it's not like I'm interested in you," he retorted, looking rather amused at himself.

"I'm impressed by the fact that you can string sentences together in a coherent fashion," Umma said, straight-faced. "Being the town drunk, I thought you might have stumbled into the ocean by now."

Dystorian let out a roaring laugh that seemed rather fake should one ask her. "I'm not always drunk," he insisted. "Sometimes I'm charming women."

"Oh, and how many of them are truly charmed?" she asked, arching her brow at the idiot before her.

She heard laughter from her sister Joan as she came to visit her. "Obaasan was always worried about you, but I think you are more than capable of holding your own," she smiled.

"Ah, Joan, you're so much prettier than your sister Umma here," Dystorian said, trying out what Umma thought he must've imagined was a charming grin.

Joan narrowed her dark eyes until they were mere slits. "My sister and I are different types of beautiful, but we both possess beauty all the same."

"You can be honest. She is uglier than the dark side of the moon," Dystorian insisted, snorting.

"Aren't you charming?" Joan snarked, rolling her eyes. "I'm a nice guy," Dystorian grinned.

Umma had enough of listening to this idiot. She didn't even know why he came to the forge if all he were going to do were insult her. Regardless of whether or not her brother-in-law had agreed to help Dystorian, she would not. She didn't care what the loss to her wages might be.

"You can leave now," Umma scowled. "I'm not sure why Hedrian agreed to help you. Perhaps, he thought he was doing you a favour, but he didn't really realize how much of a disfavour he was doing the rest of us for allowing you to be here."

"Are you refusing my services?" Dystorian asked. "My father owns half this city, Umma, I would rethink that if I were you."

"Your father may own half the city, but he doesn't own me or this forgery. I will not help you. I don't know what you're interested in other than ogling some of the girls that work here, but I am done dealing with your dumbassery."

Joan nodded. "I will tell my husband why my sister refused to work with or for you, and I'm sure he'll agree that it's worth it."

"But I'm such a nice guy," Dystorian insisted, grabbing Umma by the wrist. "You will do this—."

Umma didn't even let Dystorian finish his sentence. She didn't care how intelligent it may have been. She pulled the jade hair pins from her hair and stabbed Dystorian in the arm with them.

He recoiled instantly, as he bled upon the ground. "You little bitch," Dystorian snarled. "My blood is worth more than yours ever will be, and you go spilling it like I'm some commoner?!" He backhanded Umma so hard that she fell backward on her butt.

"LEAVE HER ALONE!" Joan snarled, pulling her knitting needles from her bag. "If you think those hurt, wait until I take your eyes with these," she snapped.

Umma stood, pulling the jade hair clips from Dystorian's arm. "Pity these used to be my favourite hair clips. With your blood now on them the price goes down. I will have to clean them carefully to get your dirty blood from every crevice of them."

Dystorian looked as if he would like to say more, but he spit in Umma's face instead.

Umma felt her teeth clench before she punched him so hard in the face his nose broke. It felt satisfying to feel it shatter beneath her palms. She pushed the hair clips into Joan's arms before she just kept punching and punching. Her sister was yelling something but she did not hear her. All Umma could see was red.

The healer checked on him, claiming that Dystorian would make a full recovery within a few days. Pity! Umma rather thought the world would've been heralding her a hero if she had successfully managed to take Dystorian out. Maybe she could summon a jade dragon to eat him or something.

Later that night after her bath, Umma thought she had heard something. Yet when she looked to confirm the presence of whatever it was that she heard, nothing was there. Frowning, Umma thought perhaps her imagination was being overactive again. Because whilst she worked here as a blacksmith, and she liked it; she dreamed of riding through the cerulean skies on the back of a jade dragon. Dragon riders weren't common, but she would find a way to make a dragon love her. She was certain of it.

As her mind ventured into her dreams, she heard something weird; but it was too late. A sack had already gone over her head, and she felt herself forcibly being dragged from the home she shared with her sister and brother-in-law and their children. She screamed to no avail. No one seemed to hear her. She felt her rage only rising with each moment. She knew that this had to be retaliation for Dystorian.

She couldn't break free with any spell or magic she tried to use which meant these bastards were probably using magic, too. She cursed beneath her breath for what had to be the hundredth time.

"Umma, you have a tongue worse than that of a sailor," one of the men scoffed. She recognized the voice. It was Dystorian's older brother, who was every bit as bad as him if not worse.

"Wasn't aware that words offended your delicate ears," Umma sneered. Because to her that's all curse words were. Words. Sure words could carry weight or meaning, but if someone was offended by a simple curse word then they were rather delicate should one ask her.

It wasn't as if she were cursing them, which was something she might try to do once she felt her magic break the threshold of theirs. She was getting a little annoyed that she couldn't free herself. She had freed herself from past attempts at kidnapping in the past, but these asses might actually be successful.

The others that were with him seemed to agree for they were all laughing, too.

"Shut up!"

Umma couldn't help but chuckle. "I'm sorry I'm more charming than you, Virgil."

"Shut up!" Virgil snapped.

Umma grimaced as she felt someone's fist collide hard with her mouth. She tasted the metallic taste of blood in her mouth. "Is that all you've got?" she sneered.

"Leave her, your father won't be happy if she's too bloodied before we get her there."

Virgil was cursing himself.

Umma felt her lips curl into a smirk. "Hypocrite!" she sneered.

"SHUT UP!" Virgil roared.

Half-an-hour later she felt them put chains around her wrists. These were magic cancelling shackles she realized, because she couldn't even think of performing a spell without feeling twinges of pain going through her body. Bastards! She saw the sky was dipping into the most beautiful shades of carnelian, ruby, and topaz interspersed with golds and pinks. Pity she was seeing it here, and not with her sister or her nieces and nephews.

The company could be much better, she thought. Slowly, she saw Dystorian and Virgil's father make his way to her. She thought it might have taken him half-a-century to get there with the pace he took.

"Ah, our esteemed guest, Umma," he crowed, massaging his moustache.

"Full of fleas?" Umma scoffed.

"Fleas? Why would it be full of fleas?" he asked, stroking his beard.

"Well, seeing as you and your sons are dogs, I thought, you might need a flea shot or potion treatment," Umma told him, with a smirk.

"Nothing can cut your spirits down, can it?" Lyrian asked, looking both a mixture of impressed and annoyed.

"Nothing," Umma agreed.

"Well, maybe this will," Lyrian snarled, shoving a hot fire poker deep into Umma's left thigh.

Umma didn't let out a sound no matter how much it hurt. The pain wouldn't get to her, she wouldn't allow them to hear her cry out in agony. The only person she had let witness that was Joan when her parents died and then when her grandmother had died. These horrid men would not hear her cry out. She wouldn't give them that satisfaction.

"Apologize," Lyrian snapped.

"For what?" Umma scoffed.

"What you said and did to my son," Lyrian insisted, tilting her chin so she had to look into his ugly blue eyes. They weren't remarkable oceans or beautiful sapphires. They weren't any pretty shade of blue. They were simply remarkable in that they were the ugliest blue eyes she had ever seen in her life.

"No," Umma insisted.

"I don't think you understand the gravity of the situation, Umma—."

Umma had discovered she could use magic again. Whatever spell these men had been using to restrain her had ended. She had never done it before, but Umma concentrated all her energy into summoning a jade dragon. She had dreamed of them since she was a child. She knew that she would see one, one day. Perhaps, they would help her today.

As if the universe had heard she had needed a helping hand, jade dragons had indeed appeared.

Umma cackled her amusement and her joy before using the men's confusion to her advantage. She used the shackles to knock them down and out of her way. As she looked to the dragons, she realized they were awaiting her instructions.

"You," she said, gently and lovingly stroking the face of the dragon nearest her. "Take me home." She then turned the rest of the dragons. "The rest of you, destroy his estate."

The dragons blinked at her slowly before obeying her commands. She felt weightless as a feather as the dragon nearest her, gently placed her on it's back before soaring through the clouds. She had never felt the soft whisper of cloud feathers against her chin, but the soft mist of water and magic against her cheeks made her feel calmer than she had in ages.

Umma grinned, she couldn't wait to tell her sister that they had pet dragons now. She turned when she saw Dystorian on a dragon of his own, his red and mean looking. He was trying to hit her dragon with a bow and arrow, she realized.

Scowling, she leaped off the back of her own dragon and shoved one of his arrows through his chest before he could even react. She then leapt off the back of the red dragon, and back onto her own green.

The dragon watched the red dragon fly off before resuming her journey forward.

Umma let out a happy sigh. As far as she was concerned, all was right in the world.

The Wyvern's Wintercearig

By Jason P Burnham

Through long dark nights
Through groves covered by downy snow
Deep into the heart of silence
And further still
Lies the sorrowful wyvern
Prostrate in its thicket
At the mercy of the cold.
The freeze so deep it's glacial
Icy blue creep
Even the warmth of a fiery belly
Struggles to keep it at bay
And flights of flickering fire
Quickly frozen back
Makes for a sad and sorry serpent
Until the summer sun
Gets reptilian ruminations
Into a brighter track.

The Water Dragon's Lark

By Stephen S Power

The Lake in Central Park, New York City

Beneath the bright reflection of Bow Bridge
a water dragon watches for a lark.
The dragon loves the way she glides and dives,
the way her wingtips flip when she alights,
how sinuous she rises and how high.
She makes him feel as clumsy as a stone.

His vision ripples as a little stone
splashes above his snout. Up on the bridge
a lady looks about, her head held high,
but turning sharply like a skittish lark.
Her dark eyes brim with tears, catching the light,
then shadows as she leans, it seems, to dive.

The dragon tenses, thinking, *Should I dive?*
Her look, though, mirrors his. He turns to stone.
He knows the weight of waiting. It's never light.
She dabs a dainty cloth along the bridge
of her fine nose. He scrapes his own. The lark
will come, she must, but she'll keep to her heights.

The lady lifts a compact's mirror high
to fix her smudged eyes. Her spirit dives
as dabbing only masks her like a lark.
She snaps it shut and drops it like a stone
into the lake, then sobs and flees the bridge.
The space where she had stood bleeds pallid light.

As if to seal this breach, into the light
a man runs glistening, his hand held high.
He looks about for someone on the bridge.
He waves. He turns. He stops. His spirit dives.
He draws a curl of metal with a stone
brighter than morning in the song of larks

out of his coat. He holds it how a lark
would grip some straw: precious for being light,
but once fixed in a nest, stronger than stone.
The dragon searches for his lark on high.
Nothing. To ease his nerves the dragon dives
and plans to help the man up on the bridge:

Being no lark, unable to fly high
to find the lady, then alight and dive,
even drop stones to drive her toward the bridge,
he finds amidst the stones beneath the bridge
her mirror, looks in it, and as light dives
he takes the lark-masked face she left behind.

Now shaped like her, he swims beside the bridge
while startled people ask if they should dive
in to assist. The man calls out, voice high
and cracking as he stumbles over stones
along the shore to grab him. Dripping light,
he stands up, shaky as a newborn lark

first thinking what it means to be a lark.
The man holds him, then helps him to a stone
where he can sit. The dragon wants to dive
back in the lake and hide beneath the bridge.
He took this shape to search the Ramble high
and low for her, not take her stone of light,

but here the man is, on a knee, the light
a dawning sun atop a metal bridge.
The dragon sees why birds like shiny stones.
Maybe with this one, he could draw his lark,
the way it has a crowd who just might dive
off the old bridge, waiting to hear the high

soft breath of yes. Past them he sees, yes, high
over the lake, wagging its wings, the lark.
She swoops and makes him look north of the bridge:
The lady's coming back. His head feels light
as he leaps up, pushes away the stone,
hears everybody groan, then spins and dives

into the lake. Beneath the bridge he dives

into himself again, awhirl in light.
Perching within an arabesque, the lark
is mesmerized. Her heart has long been high
on him, but could not bear to cross the bridge
of saying so. *You cannot soar with stones,*

she thinks, but how he glides amidst the stones.
He was so brave to come, for him, on high,
and shed those scales, those wondrous shards of light.
She's soared so long. It's time to really dive.
And as the dragon looks up at the lark,
the man holds up his stone up on Bow Bridge.

The Dragon's Bite
By Matias F Travieso-Diaz

As the rays of the sun pounded on the surface of the dry lake, an egg cracked open, sending leathery shards flying in all directions.

The wyrmling shook himself free of egg remnants and slid onto the hardened muck. He was small, less than three feet from muzzle to tail, and had trouble keeping his eyes open in the blazing afternoon light. His instincts told him that something was wrong. He should have awakened immersed in cool, dark waters replete with swimming food. He was hungry, but nothing edible seemed to lie within the thrust of his tongue. He began to slither towards the shore.

A couple of times along the way he attempted to fly. His wings, however, were still pinned to his flanks and hardly stirred when he made a gesture with his shoulders to unfurl them. He let out an exasperated howl, a ragged cry for help. Where was his mother?

He reached the shore of what once had been a deep body of water. Except for desiccated shrubs covered with dust, there were no signs that life had ever existed in this corner of the world. Yet, he smelled a living being of some kind a little distance away. He moved clumsily at first, digging his clawed feet into the pebbles that covered the ground. As the scent of prey became more pronounced, the wyrmling picked up speed and in a few seconds reached the top of a rise from which he could see the prairie below. A skinny four-legged animal, slightly larger than him, was grazing at a clump of yellowed grass.

The wyrmling's next actions were automatic. He ran towards the animal, inhaling big gulps of air, contorted, and emitted a very thin ray of incandescent gas towards his victim. The animal had already detected peril and started to run away, but the flame caught up to it in a moment and singed its legs, forcing it to the ground. The wyrmling kept spitting fire at the prone animal, and when the two were next to each other, the predator jumped onto his partly carbonized victim, held it between his forelegs, and started taking huge chunks of flesh with his two rows of sharp teeth.

It was all over in a matter of seconds. The wyrmling consumed every bit of his victim down to the fragile bones. He let out a satisfied grunt and lowered himself to the ground to digest his meal and take his first nap since birth.

***

His exploration of the barren land continued when he arose. There was nothing to see for a good distance but, far away to the west, he came upon a clump of timbered structures arranged in a semicircle around a hole in the ground from which rose the remembered smell of water. Thirst more than curiosity drew the wyrmling towards the hole. He was nearly there when he felt motion around him, as creatures that stood on two legs began emerging from the wooden structures. Cries resonated and the air filled with projectiles aimed at him. One of those hit the wyrmling on the back of the head. It did not quite penetrate the hard scales that covered his body, but the projectile exploded on his hide, burning it and causing him to scamper for cover, fleeing to safety among the loud noises emitted by his attackers.

He marked the bipeds as enemies and vowed to come after them as soon as he could.

***

Over the next several moons, the wyrmling managed to survive in the barren land. He preyed on birds by downing them off the air with blasts of fire, swallowed crawling creatures that failed to escape his pursuit, ate carrion left behind by other predators. His keen sense of smell allowed him to find oases and pools that held muddy waters, but both the meager food and the foul waters left him unsatisfied. He felt he had to get more and better sustenance if he was going to grow to his full potential. These needs went largely unmet, but he grew rapidly nonetheless.

In one of his forays, he came across a lone biped accompanied by half a dozen four-legged animals like the one that had served as his first meal. He made a quick calculation: he could down several of the four-legged animals or go after the biped. Resentment dictated his choice, and he charged at the biped and carbonized him with an angry blast. Turning to

the four-legged creatures, he managed to roast a couple before
the others dispersed.

He turned his attention to the fallen biped. The victim's body
was mostly charred but several morsels of intact anatomy
remained. The wyrmling bit into those, reveling in
anticipation of sweet meat and revenge.

He found the biped's meager flesh disappointing. It was
stringy, dry, and almost flavorless. It was also marred by a
lingering undertaste of unnatural substances that revolted him.
Whatever these bipeds were, their bodies were deeply
polluted and unfit for consumption. He would kill them if the
occasion presented itself, but would not partake of their flesh
again.

***

Half a cycle around the sun after his hatching, the wyrmling
– now a dragonet – had grown into a twenty foot of terror
capable of swooping out of the sky like a bolt of lightning onto
an unsuspecting prey. There were few wild animals left in the
empty lands he called home, but he lorded over all of them
and had developed a particular predilection for the four-legged
beasts tended to by the bipeds. He played a game of hit and
run in which he would come close enough to the biped's
habitations to taunt them and steal one or two of the animals
they kept, and then fly away out of reach of their projectiles.
Through repeated contacts, he had learned some of the bipeds'
language, who called themselves "humans" and referred to the
dragonet as "L'ong." To the humans, L'ong was a deadly

threat, to be destroyed if possible but warded against by all possible means.

As he grew to adult size, L'ong developed into a daunting figure. He had a powerful, spiky tail, enormous wings whose span extended twice the length of his red body, a skin reinforced by armored scales containing tiny bones that functioned as a natural chain-mail, razor sharp serrated teeth that measured a couple of inches in length, and a long, forked tongue that he used to detect, smell, and taste those objects that came within its reach. He had loosely articulated jaws that now allowed him to swallow, in a single bite, animals almost the size of humans.

He loathed the midday heat that was always present in this blasted land, so he only hunted at dawn and near sunset, and sometimes at night. His silhouette, appearing like a sudden dark blot in the sky, sent humans into a panic, forcing them to seek refuge in the underground shelters they had to construct once L'ong started to visit their village.

***

Despite their precautions, humans never remained unscathed whenever L'ong paid them a call. The terror the dragon inspired and the bloody toll he exacted forced the inhabitants of the villages to think of ways of setting traps to capture him before he wiped out their entire population. A resident of one of the settlements came up with a plan: "Let's start paying L'ong a tribute. We'll sacrifice animals to him so he will leave the rest of us alone."

The plan was not well received at first, until its proponent clarified: "At some point, the sacrificial animal could be poisoned."

Initially the plan was carried without a glitch. L'ong feasted on a pig chosen for its relative plumpness compared to other emaciated domestic animals. He did not return for a week or so, but when he did the humans were ready. They placed in the middle of the village common a calf that had been fed a blend of poisonous herbs and could barely stand. L'ong descended in front of the offering, examined him with his sensitive tongue, issued a harsh cry of disgust, and directed a wall of flame at the calf and the three nearest huts, turning all to cinders.

The humans were discouraged by this setback, but came up with another plan. "We won't feed him poison, but our sacrificial offerings will be the sickest among our cattle. Perhaps he will eat them and fall sick himself."
The modified plan was put into effect shortly thereafter. The next offering was a goat that was near death from affliction with black quarter disease. The goat was breathing with difficulty and exhibiting swelling of the hip, back and shoulder due to the internal accumulation of gas. L'ong landed next to the animal, examined it carefully with his tongue, and took a huge bite of the goat's back. He did not swallow the morsel, however. He spat the flesh and flew away after burning to the ground half a dozen huts.

When it was clear that the dragon was gone for the evening, the village's inhabitants advanced gingerly to the place where the goat lay, writhing in pain. Then they made a startling discovery: the goat was bleeding profusely from the dragon's bite, but the body swelling was disappearing and the animal appeared to breathe more normally, though in fits and starts from the pain.

They picked the goat up and took it back to its pen, keeping it isolated from other animals.

Three days later, a scar was forming at the site of the dragon's bite and the animal was back on its feet, bleating as if all was well.

"It's a miracle," said some humans.

Others of a more scientific bent hypothesized: "There may be something in L'ong's saliva that cured whatever was causing the disease. We need to investigate this further."

Further modifications were made to the human's plan for dealing with L'ong. The site of the sacrifices was moved to an altar built on a hillock some distance from the village, to try to avoid further dwelling incinerations, and the offerings were made in the evening. Once a week, animals were presented for sacrifice suffering from a variety of cattle diseases: foot and mouth, rinderpest, even a suspected early attack of anthrax. L'ong devoured some of the offerings, flew away with disdain at others, took a bite or two of other victims before going away. In all cases, an animal that was left alive after being bitten by the dragon managed to recover.

"What are we going to do now?" asked a human. "It seems that L'ong's bite will cure some diseases, but we don't know if it will work on all, plus he is still eating our animals and destroying our homes."

A heavy silence followed, broken at last by an old man: "Something is gnawing at my innards, and I feel more exhausted each day. I don't think I have much left to live. I'll offer myself as a sacrifice to the dragon."

***

They tried hard to dissuade him from his suicidal plan, but at the end they allowed the old man to place himself on the sacrificial altar each night, awaiting L'ong's arrival. On the fourth night the dragon swooped down from the sky, approached the hillock, glanced at the sprawled offering, and veered away. As he parted, L'ong issued three guttural words: "No eat humans."

"Wait!" replied the old man, getting up from the altar. "I don't want you to eat me, just to take a bite!"

L'ong stopped in mid-flight and returned to the ground. "Why?" he asked suspiciously.

"I'm very sick" replied the old man, "and something in your bite may cure me, as it did some of our animals. Please give it a try."

L'ong moved next to the old man. "I do this only once." The dragon bit sharply below the old man's shoulder, almost severing an arm. The man screamed and fainted.

A week later, an old man with a heavy bandage on his shoulder led a discussion of the leaders of his village on how to deal with L'ong. "I declare, other than the wound on my shoulder, I feel as good as I did when I was a youngster." His wife nodded her head, a knowing smile on her lips.

"We are all glad about your recovery, but we can't beg this monster to come bite every sick person in this town. After all, most of us have some form of death working its way inside us."

"Why not?" replied the old man. "The worst that can happen is that he will bite us and the disease will kill us all the same. We have nothing really to lose except for a painful bite by those teeth. I say we find a way to persuade L'ong to work with us on this."

***

One evening later in the week, there were two victims lying on the altar: a young, emaciated woman who hardly moved at all and a lamb that fought energetically to free itself from the ropes that kept it tied to the altar's supports.

"What this?" questioned L'ong as he hovered above the scene.

The old man L'ong had bitten in their previous encounter joined the couple at the altar and replied: "Your bite cured me, and we want you to do the same for many of our kin who suffer from disease. In exchange, we'll give you a healthy animal to enjoy for each human you help."

L'ong lacked the ability to formulate a verbal reply to this offer, but substituted action for words. He approached the young woman and bit her on the neck gently. He then cleansed his mouth by spitting into the ground and yanked the lamb from its bindings, swallowed it whole in a single motion, and took off, a patch of deeper darkness against the night sky.

A strange form of commerce then developed between dragon and humans. L'ong's bite cured many, but not all, the humans who presented themselves for treatment. There was no explanation why some "patients" failed to respond to the dragon's ministrations, but their demise was accepted as a limitation in an imperfect medical practice. After all, sometimes not even the potent kiss of a dragon can push death away.

The village started to prosper as its inhabitants regained good health and energy, though the livestock losses were grievous.

Everything seemed fine until one evening in the early spring of the following year. L'ong appeared late, yanked a lamb off the altar, ate it in a single gulp, and prepared to leave, ignoring the trembling man that had been waiting for L'ong's bite.

"Are you leaving without treating me?" asked the man querulously.

L'ong's final words were lost as he rose to the skies: "Need to find mate."

He was never seen again in that village or any other human settlement in the entire area. His story has become another legend among the folks who scratch a living in the inhospitable prairie. "Not even dragons like to live here" is often the melancholy conclusion of L'ong's tale.

But others retort, forgetting L'ong's depredations: "But it was good while it lasted." For mankind is always capable of finding a bit of good even in the most dreadful events.

Chema Valdez and the Terror of the Sierra Madre

By Jibril Stevenson

It was mid-November and Chema Valdez was glad to be migrating south for the winter. He'd already had his fill of ice and snow in Alaska, not to mention hairy dog-men, hairier bushmen and a couple of man-eating bears, so he had jumped at the chance to head down Mexico way.

It wasn't just the weather, of course. How long had it been since he'd been among his own people, spoken his own language, eaten pozole like mamá used to make? He was an American citizen, having been born in south Texas shortly after Taylor and his bluecoats manifested their destiny all over the Rio Grande valley, but Chema had never felt quite comfortable among the gabachos. Mexico would be like a homecoming for his soul.

His destination was the Montezuma Gold Mine deep in the Sierra Madre. Several miners had disappeared in its labyrinthine passages, and the mine's owners—an English joint-stock company—did not want to involve the police, who probably received a monthly payment to ignore the miserable working conditions and suppress any stirrings of trade unionism. Anyway, the miners were convinced it wasn't a human murderer picking them off one by one, but rather a fearsome monster.

And monsters were Chema's specialty.

***

A four-thousand-mile voyage was never easy, especially not when a good portion of it was by dogsled or fishing boat or burro, but he reached Zacatecas eventually, no worse for wear, just a few days shy of Christmas. The caserío of Santa Bárbara de los Mineros turned out to be little more than a dozen wind-worn adobe shacks clustered at the mouth of a narrow draw carved into the side of an imposing ridge of bare granite.

One of the shacks had a sign hanging above the door, bearing a crude painting of a snake that on closer inspection turned out to be a maguey worm. Chema went in and ordered a mezcal and a plate of pozole. Since landing in Mazatlán, he'd had enough of both to quench his nostalgia, but it felt like a sin to forgo the opportunity.

"Are you Señor Valdez?" asked the barman as he filled Chema's glass. They were alone in the dingy cantina, except for an ancient Indian who was stirring up the fire to reheat the pot of pozole.

Chema nodded. He wasn't surprised to be recognized. He'd come by invitation after all, and his American clothes— cowhand's Stetson, sheepskin coat, denim trousers, and a pistol belt with a single Smith and Wesson .44—must've given him away. Hell, he was probably the first stranger to visit this remote village in months, anyway.

The barman spoke a few words in some Indian tongue, and the old man left off poking at the fire and shambled out into the street. Turning his attention back to Chema, the barman said, "The Englishman expected you yesterday."

Not surprising. The damned English expected everything to run on the same timetables as the London Underground. Chema gestured for the man to bring his pozole, which must be at least lukewarm by now, and settled in to wait for the mine's representative to arrive.

Punctual as the 5:30 train, Mr. Shirley Hibblethwaite—for that was the Englishman's unfortunate name—strolled in a minute later, the poor Indian struggling to keep up.

"Mister Valdez," he shouted in his peculiar dialect, "you're late."

Chema didn't have much patience for this gringo's pendejadas. He could have walked right out, got back on his burro and ridden down to Guerrero where his services were needed to deal with a shapeshifting nagual, and one day he'd probably wish he had. But the Montezuma was a literal gold mine, and the promised reward was too good to pass up.

So Chema shook the Englishman's limp, pale hand and they sat to discuss the latest news from the mine.

"There have been seven more fatalities since last we corresponded," said Hibblethwaite. "Same as before. Spatters of blood. No bodies."

Chema mused a few seconds. "Might be some kind of duende. Like your tommyknockers and the kobolds of

Europe. The chaneques around here live in the forests, not the mines, but—"

"Mister Valdez," said Hibblethwaite, cutting him off. At least his Britannic formality would preclude him addressing Chema as "Joe" like the other gringos did. "My miners weren't killed by some local hobgoblins. They believe it was a beast they call Tehuancoatl."

Upon hearing that word, the two Indians crossed themselves, though they had given no indication of eavesdropping and certainly spoke no English.

Chema was part Indian himself, but his mamá was from Tamaulipas, where no jaguar-clad Aztec had ever set foot. Still, even she had heard of Tehuancoatl. "The 'vile serpent'," Chema said, remembering the stories of his childhood. "Usually such creatures dwell in water. Does the mine tap any subterranean lakes or rivers?"

The Englishman shrugged. "There are miles of tunnels, Mister Valdez. Who knows what's down there?"

***

When they reached the mine itself, Chema saw that the Englishman had not been exaggerating.

From the entrance, which was a rather uninspiring rectangular gap hacked into the rock at the top of the draw, they walked down a short tunnel, wide and deep enough to stand upright and well lit with kerosene lamps, and emerged into a vast gallery. The gallery looked to be a natural cavern, with crystalline stalactites hanging from the ceiling, but the floor had been flattened, and scores of miners surged this way and that, pushing handcarts full of ore or spoil, crushing great piles of ore with sledgehammers or wearing the rocks away with jets of water pumped up from some hidden source, or standing waist-deep in noxious pools to sift miniscule pebbles of gold from the dross.

"We diverted the stream," said Hibblethwaite, noting Chema's interest in the waterworks. "The water drains through a culvert and down to Santa Bárbara. We wouldn't want the villagers to be thirsty."
Chema grimaced at the thought of drinking the oily liquid.

The overwhelming majority of the miners were Indians, but only a few looked to be local Huicholes or Zacatecos. The rest were short-statured Mayas, probably captured by the Mexican army in the Yucatán, where the Race War had been ongoing for years. Mestizo guards and overseers armed with cudgels patrolled at strategic intervals around the gallery, ready to punish any slacker or thief on the spot.

"Listen up!" shouted Hibblethwaite in decent Spanish. "This is Señor Valdez, the famous monster-killer. He will track down your Tehuancoatl."

The miners all crossed themselves, and most of the guards did too. They watched Chema with a mixture of admiration and pity as he made his way through the mine. Hibblethwaite called over one of the guards, an ex-soldier who introduced himself as Sergeant Pérez, and instructed him to show Chema where the killings had occurred.

Chema and the sergeant spent the rest of the day walking—and sometimes crawling—down the tunnels, looking for the precise locations where each miner had last been seen. The tunnels, even when spacious enough to stand upright, grew more and more claustrophobic as they descended deeper underground. The air was heavy and stale, the darkness oppressive, overpowering the weak orange light that barely emanated from the sergeant's lantern.

The first spot was as described in Hibblethwaite's letter months ago: no sign of violence except for a splattering of blood on the rock. Sergeant Pérez said the unfortunate victim had been the last man in a crew of miners filing back toward the gallery at the end of the day, and that he hadn't cried out. It was only the clattering of his pickaxe on the stone floor that alerted his fellows that anything was amiss. Chema lit an electric candle to inspect the surroundings in near-daylight, but found no additional clues.

The second site was more informative. This particular stretch of access tunnel had been dug through softer rock, and Chema's white light revealed strange marks scratched into walls and floor. They came in threes—claw marks.
This wasn't some overgrown cave snake. It was something else entirely.

Chema paced off the intervals between claw marks, and measured the distance between the individual claws. The creature must be enormous, bigger than anything Chema had ever seen.

He turned off the electric light so Pérez wouldn't see the grin spreading across his face.

Chema had never slain a dragon before.

The Englishman had been predictably incredulous of Chema's theory and reluctant to provide the required labor and materials, but Chema was adamant. Whether Hibblethwaite believed in dragons or not was his own concern, but Chema wasn't about to face one alone and armed with nothing but his Smith and Wesson. If Hibblethwaite didn't give him what he needed, he'd walk.

The Englishman caved.

The mining engineers drew Chema a rough map of the tunnels, and he and Sergeant Pérez marked the location and time of every death. Chema stared at the map till his eyes glazed over, unable to find a pattern in the chaos. But after observing the work in the gallery, he realized that the answer had been right under his nose.

At one end of the gallery was a short tunnel leading to a vertical shaft where all the runoff from the mine ended up, conducted by a vast series of natural fissures and narrow pipes and gutters not shown on the engineering plans. Unlike other mines, this one never required pumping to keep from flooding. Typically, the bottom of such a shaft would be scraped periodically for the gold-bearing sediment that would accumulate there.

"We've never actually reached the bottom," one of the engineers told Chema, crossing himself as he did so. "It might go all the way to Hell for all we know."

Chema decided to test that theory, but first he had a number of other preparations to make. He and a small group of trustworthy miners spent all night working at the mouth of the shaft, and in the connecting tunnel before Chema was ready to risk a descent.

Suspended by the longest, strongest chain they could find him, attached to a leather harness around his waist and thighs, Chema inched downward into the black abyss. The miners' torches soon vanished from view as the deathly darkness enveloped him.

A soft, warm breeze blew him this way and that, telling him he was no longer in a narrow shaft, but rather in a cavern of unknown dimensions. It was as utterly black as the prison cell in Poe's story, with Chema playing the part of the pendulum, but he did not despair, for he knew he must be close to his quarry.

"¡Tehuancoatl!" he shouted. "Come out, come out, wherever you are!"

The warm breeze grew stronger, and a deep rumble came from the depths, reverberating from the walls of the cavern. His ears perceived no sound, but Chema felt the roar in the marrow of his bones, seismic and animal at once, and then he heard the voice.

Again, his ears were cheated of their role for the voice insinuated itself directly into Chema's brain. It was a presence so malignant, so alien that Chema released his grip on the chains and pounded his hands against his ears, trying to expel the strange sibilant susurrations.

The voice resolved itself into words in Chema's mind. It was not English, not Spanish nor Huasteca, but Chema understood.

"Who dares disturb us in our abode?"

"I am José María Valdez," he answered, trying to keep his voice from catching. His words disappeared into the void, too weak to echo.

"Ah, the 'dragon-slayer'…" There was an inhuman sound between a hiss and a growl that must have been the creature's caricature of laughter.

Chema didn't know what he'd expected, but it wasn't this. Still, he wasn't about to let some overgrown salamander make a fool of him. He tugged on the chain and was relieved to feel his body slowly rise.

"And who are you?" he asked, his voice less shaky this time.

"Did you not call us by name? We are the vile serpent Tehuancoatl, yes, and we are the feathered serpents Quetzalcoatl and Kukulkan. We are Fafnir and Nidhoggr, Apophis, Dagon and Tiamat, Behemoth and Leviathan. We are Mictlantecuhtli, too, ruler of the down below, and we are Huitzilopochtli, to whom emperors once made sacrifice…"

Chema's mind filled with images of roaring flame and rivers or blood, teeth and claws and leathery wings, then still-beating hearts torn from human breasts, lifeless bodies tumbling down the steps of great pyramids, mounds of sun-bleached bones and towers of grinning skulls, and above it all the dragon's evil eye…

Nearly overcome by the vision, Chema could not find the words to reply, but the beast continued all the same.

"We do not demand so much blood now, only a few poor Indians in exchange for the riches of our realm. But if you think to break our bargain, we will not be so restrained…"

Chema shook himself out of his daze, seizing the chain in a white-knuckled grip. Though he could feel himself ascending as fast as the miners could raise him, Chema began to climb hand-over-hand like a monkey, desperate to get back to the surface.

For he had sensed rather than heard from deep below the scratching of claws, the scraping of scales on bare rock and the beating of wings in the darkness.

The scraping ceased and the wingbeats grew stronger, closer. The warm breeze has become a fierce wind, like the steam from a furnace. Looking down, Chema still saw only darkness, but when he looked up, he was relieved to see the glimmer of distant torches.

He climbed faster and faster, though his shoulders ached. The torchlight grew brighter until Chema could make out the anxious faces of the miners who were hauling him up.

The wingbeats had ceased, replaced anew by the scratching of claws on rock. Tehuancoatl was climbing the narrow shaft now, too close for Chema's comfort, but unable to move as swiftly as before. The air was still except for the beast's steamy breath, stinking of sulfur and carrion.

With a clatter of chains, the miners pulled Chema over the edge. They had barely unfastened his harness when a powerful blast of air knocked them to the ground. Some screamed and some ran, while others stood still, transfixed by the terrible sight before them. Chema scrambled to his feet, grabbing a fallen torch to illuminate the face of Tehuancoatl.

The head came first, tapered and scaly, with horns like a viper, but lined with ragged feathers. It opened its maw to reveal rows of razor sharp teeth. The stench of death filled the tunnel.

"Run, little dragon-slayer. Run while you still can." That's exactly what Chema did.

looked over his shoulder just long enough to see the dragon's jaws close on one of the miners who hadn't had the sense to flee. It tossed the poor man's corpse aside, clearly not interested in feeding, but only in killing.

It was halfway out of the shaft now, pulling itself up with massive, taloned claws. Its wings were visible too, still folded, the vestigial claws at their tips gleaming in the torchlight. It let out a blood-curdling roar.

Chema dove into the shallow trench he had ordered dug the night before and waved the torch around, looking for the weaponry he had hidden there. A few yards away, where the tunnel joined the main gallery, there was a loud explosion and then the rumble of falling rock.

For better or for worse, they had followed Chema's instructions to seal the tunnel. They should have sealed the other tunnels already, assuming Hibblethwaite had bought Chema's assurances that the work stoppage would last no more than two days.

Chema was alone with the dragon Tehuancoatl. Just as he wanted.

The beast had freed itself from the narrow shaft and was advancing down the tunnel toward Chema, sniffing and snuffling like a bloodhound.

"You should have run," it said. "You cannot hide from us for long." It punctuated its sentence with an image of jaws and teeth, blood spraying in all directions from a body Chema could only imagine must be his own.

He took a deep breath, counted to three, and stood up, using his foot to cock the crossbow he had hidden in the trench.

It was not quite deep enough for a grave, as Chema had joked to the miners, but the trench was deep enough that only his head and shoulders protruded. He set the crossbow on the ground in front of him, making sure the beast would hear the crack of wood on stone.

Tehuancoatl turned toward the sound and fixed its flame-red eyes on Chema. With a movement more lizard-like than serpentine, it approached his hiding place.
Transferring the torch to his left hand, Chema drew his revolver fast as any gunfighter and started shooting. The silver bullets bounced off the monster's shimmering scales, some of them striking sparks as they ricocheted off the tunnel walls.

"Your pea-shooter will not hurt me, dragon-slayer." The beast laughed its weird hiss-roar, opening its maw wider than Chema could have imagined possible.

Just as he had hoped.

Chema grabbed the crossbow and pulled the trigger, launching an arrow straight down the dragon's throat. Then he ducked back into his trench and prayed to the Virgen de Guadalupe.

Tehuancoatl screamed and choked for exactly one second, before the five-second fuse ran out on the half dozen sticks of dynamite embedded just below its uvula.

The explosion rocked the whole mine and sent chunks of dragon-flesh flying in all directions. A torrent of steaming blood filled Chema's trench, bathing him in the foul substance.

Suddenly wearier than he'd ever been, Chema dragged himself out of the hole and waded through dragon guts to reach the vertical shaft. He peered over the edge and saw only darkness.

But Chema was not fooled. The malignant presence had not left his mind when the dynamite blew Tehuancoatl into a million pieces.

"We are still Tehuancoatl, yes," said the voice, "and we are Quetzalcoatl and Kukulkan. We are Fafnir and Nidhoggr, Apophis, Dagon and Tiamat, Behemoth and Leviathan…"

Chema lit the fuse dangling from the ceiling, where he and a few trustworthy miners had secured a half-ton of dynamite behind a chicken-wire net. Then he ducked back into his trench and shimmied through the escape tunnel, so narrow he had to take his hat and gun-belt off to fit through, until he met the terrified miners on the other side.

***

"What in bloody Hell were you thinking?" demanded Hibblethwaite.

The explosion had collapsed half the mountain; the Montezuma Gold Mine would operate at a loss for years to come, if the British joint-stock company even decided to keep it running.

"I can't in good conscience pay your fee after what you've done."

Chema grinned and rested his hand theatrically on the grip of his Smith and Wesson. "I don't only kill monsters, you know."

In the end, the gringo paid him, and Chema was happy enough. He had money in his pocket, and there was still that nagual to hunt down in Guerrero. He tried not to think about the Hell of fire and vile monsters teeming just below ground, barely held back by a few hundred yards of rubble.

After all, he only heard the dragons' voice at night.

The Dragon Behind the Door

By Alex Souza

When Tariq opened the door, there was no dragon on the other side.

"Thank God," he murmured, "it's just a home."

Tariq asked himself when was the last time he had opened a door to a regular house—did he ever? Following the Librarian through the multiverse always led Tariq to the most bizarre situations: dungeons deep into the Earth, castles full of vampires; parallel universes where people had sausages for fingers, or guns for heads; sometimes, you just walked into the mouth of a dragon. Weirdly enough, an old house was a first. He had followed the Librarian to a grove, and got lost. The door was in the middle of the grove—with no house around it, just the door.

The boy closed his eyes and breathed a great sigh of relief, but a smell caught his attention. *Smells like soil, like a mine…* he thought, sniffing the air.

Tariq felt his nose itching and sneezed, making particles of dust float in the air, illuminated only by the dim light that came from the holes on the gray walls. Covering his nose, he began walking toward the bedroom, but froze when he felt something sharp nudging his back. Tariq swallowed hard; he knew it was a knife.

"Turn around," said the voice behind him. "Slowly."

It was a woman's voice, so hoarse that sent a shiver up Tariq's spine. He raised his hands and turned around, ready to see the wrinkled face of a witch looking down on him, but gasped when saw nothing—that is, until he lowered his head and saw the little girl.

She had pale skin and ashy hair, despite obviously being a child. There was a blood stain on the cloth that covered her mouth and nose.

She's scarier than a witch, Tariq thought.

"Why did you get in here?" the girl said. "Nobody ever gets in here. No one. At all."

"I…" Tariq found it hard to talk with a blade on his throat. "I just opened the door."

"Why?!"

"I just wanted to see what was on the other side."

"Just that? Who does that?"

"I do. I feel trapped if I don't. 'You have to break in to get out', that's my motto."

But you—" The girl suddenly moved away, eyes agape. "Why… Why are you without a mask? The plague! It's going to kill you! Leave now!"

Tariq's jaw dropped. *Has she lost it?*

"There's no plague anymore," he said. "That was more than a year ago. The ashes from the fire that the dragons spat were the cause. The Librarian helped us get rid of them." Tariq scowled. "And who wears masks inside the house anyway?"

"You lie! The Librarian abandoned us!"

"What? No! Why would he do that?"

Tariq saw the girl giving him the once over. He knew that he was dirty from running in forests, crawling in sewers and squeezing through greased cables of engine rooms. But he didn't have the plague. He was sure of that.

"The truth is that the Librarian—" The girl started to cough. She coughed so hard she had to bend over and drop the knife.

"Hey… Are you OK?"

"Of course not… Can't breathe…" She pointed to a box on the table. "Need my medicine…"

Tariq leaped to the box. Inside of it, he saw many glass flasks, but just one was full. He promptly took it to the girl.

She took off the mask, revealing bluish-gray lips, and chugged on the flask. Then, she pulled the inhaler that she had hanging from a string on her neck and breathed through it.

While the girl was breathing deeply, Tariq looked at the hair on her clothes, so thin that they were almost imperceptible. *Her hair is thinning out,* he thought. *Just like what happened to mom. But how?*

"How many are left?" The girl asked.

Tariq looked away for a while, afraid to answer, then said: "None."

"Oh…" She lowered her head and covered her face with both hands.

And started crying.

"I'm gonna die! Just like mommy, I'm gonna die!"

"Did your… Did your mom die of the plague?"

The girl nodded.

"And your dad?"

She shook her head negatively.

"But… How do you still live then?" The girl snuffled. "Your Librarian was here. He's a farce. He left me with a box full of medicine just to torture me." She wiped her nose. "I have had no food for days. The water I take from the rain."

"So why don't you just leave?"

"Isn't it obvious? Because a dragon may kill me!"

Tariq heard himself shriek. He tried to speak—his mouth opened, but nothing came out. It was like he just couldn't process that.

"Don't… Don't be stupid," he managed to say. "The dragons were all hunted down! The quarantine has been lifted and no one is sick anymore!"

"You lie! There is a dragon behind that door and you want it to kill me!"

Tariq sighed. He clenched his teeth and grabbed the girl by the wrist.

"Ow, let me go!" she shouted.

"I'll show you that there's no dragon out the… AH!" Tariq felt the pain on his arm and released the girl. He saw the blood dripping. "You…"

Tariq froze. The girl had the knife on her own throat now; some blood was already going down.

"Please," the girl said, eyes tearing up. "Don't feed me to the dragon… Anything but that…"

"But…" Now Tariq's eyes were tearing up. "I just came from outside. There's no dragon…"

"That's because they're tricky," she was whispering now. "They hide, but I know they're there. I know it. I listen to their whispers every day. They're just behind the door and I know it." She put the knife down and started to weep.

Tariq ripped some of his clothing and covered the cut on his arm, said: "What's your name?"

The girl snuffled. "Anabia…"

"Listen, Anabia, I'll go to the Librarian myself. I can follow his tracks… for a time." Tariq shrugged, said: "Maybe he still has some medicine." He walked to the door and, before opening it, turned around. "And then, I'll get you out of here. One way or the other."

***

As soon as Tariq stepped outside, he closed his eyes and felt the fresh air of the grove. He turned around and took a glance at the gray door of Anabia's house. The difference in tone was like going from black and white to Technicolor. He picked the chalk from his pocket to mark the door, but stopped. *I don't think I'll forget this door,* he thought.

Tariq then ran through the grove, following the tracks he had left behind. He passed by the doors he had marked before: the door that went to a rave party at a nightclub (the grove was the restroom), the one that was right below a waterfall, and the one that led to a chocolate factory. He would've marked this last one as a permanent return if the Librarian's portals didn't disappear after a while.

The trail of twigs was just like he had left them, so he followed it to the giant tree with a door underneath it, and picked the lock.

The ear pain confirmed that he was in the right place; he started to chew a bubble gum to stop it. He felt like a soldier crawling on mud while passing through the cables. Outside the engine room, a crew member almost saw him, but Tariq managed to hide. The passenger corridor was dark—everybody was asleep—, so he passed through with ease. Inside the cockpit, the pilot was also asleep. Tariq found the small door below the control panel and opened it with the lockpick. Before leaving, the boy didn't resist taking a look at the curvature of the Earth through the window.

As soon as he unlocked the door, the wind opened it with a bang, almost knocking Tariq down, and a light made him cover his eyes. He forced his way in and fell into the water. When he managed to stand up, he realized he was on the boat, and that he had almost drowned in a puddle.

There was a storm. The lightning was the only light source. A wave hit the vessel and Tariq almost fell on the sea. He then saw the old man holding onto the mast.

"Ahab!" Tariq shouted. The man didn't listen, so he shouted again, louder: "Captain Ahab!"

The old man saw him. "Lockpick boy! Me's embarrassed to say that me's happy to sees ye again! This captain needs the door to the sewers open again!"

"That's where I'm going!" Another wave hit the boat, and Tariq almost fell into the sea. "Help me get to the other side of the deck!"

Captain Ahab threw a rope at Tariq. "Hold that! Me doesn't let ye fall!"

Fighting against the wind and the raindrops that hit him like razors, Tariq got to the door.

"Thanks, captain!"

"Nay! Me's the one to thank ye! Now open this door lest I drown!"

The stench of the sewers almost made Tariq puke. Another wave hit the boat, and hell face-first in the brown water. The flow was stronger than before, so Tariq had to hold on to the cockroach-riddled pipe so as not to fall again. He followed the pipe to the end, until he got to the center of the sewers, which he called the Waterfalls of Sewage. He squeezed through the rusty grating and held onto the ladder. He started climbing it, paying attention to the numbers marked on the walls— seventeen, eighteen, nineteen—until he got to the twentieth, the one he had marked.

He squeezed through the grating, entered pipe #20 and saw the marked door. He had a smile on his face, ready to find the Librarian and set Anabia free. But when he tried to pick the door's lock, he realized he was pushing his lockpick into metal.

"Uh-oh," he said. He smelled tobacco and saw smoke where the door should've been. "It was just here…just this instant."

A growl sent shivers up his spine. Something was coming for him from deep in the pipe, each step shaking the ground. Tariq saw two yellow eyes in the darks, and then the scales, the thick green skin… the mouth full of sharp teeth.

"Dragon!" Tariq fell on his butt and skittered back until he hit the grating. He felt his heart pounding, his nape sweaty, the hands clammy. As he squeezed his body through the grating, he thought about Anabia. Without him, that girl was done for, just the way his mother was before the Librarian. Then his lockpick fell from his pocket. He watched as it fell into the sewage. *Great, now the only way is forward,* he thought, turning around to face the dragon. *You gotta break in to break out.*

He bolted towards the monster, leaped to it and bear-hugged its jaw shut.

"Ha! You're quite strong to close your mouth, but not so much to open it, huh?!"

The monster lashed out, contorted his body and did everything to make the boy let go.

Tariq clenched his teeth and held on tight, until he finally slipped. He was thrown to the wall, and his body slouched on the dirty floor.

As the monster walked towards him, mouth wide open, Tariq closed his eyes and thought about his mom. Thought about Anabia, and prayed that someone would help her get the strength to leave her house and face the world.

He looked into the dragon's mouth; looked into the darkness. It was just like back then, when he walked right into it. But back then, somebody had pulled him back.
Tariq heard the sound of a door opening. He felt a violent pull, and he got away from the darkness.

He found himself in a bathroom. He saw that it was the Library's bathroom. Because when he looked to the one that had saved him, he saw the Librarian.

"Mr. Librarian! Sir!" Tariq hugged the man and started to cry.

"Why are you crying, little man?"

Tariq stepped back and bit his lip. "That was… There was a… a dragon back there!"

"Oh, you mean George? He's an alligator. He guards the sewers. The sewage company asked me to put him there." The Librarian pulled a luxurious wooden pipe from his satchel.

"The door! The door was gone when I tried to enter it. Why?!" Tariq demanded.

"Because I'm leaving, Tariq. The Library has to move. It can't stay here forever."

"But…" Tariq gave the Librarian the once-over. The Librarian was wearing leather boots, had a cape around his body and a turban on his head. He had cut his beard and had a well-done mustache now. "Why?"

"Take a shower first. Come to my office and we'll talk." The Librarian smoked on his pipe, then blew smoke in the air.

"But…"

"Be quick." The Librarian opened a door that had just appeared among the smoke. He entered it and closed it behind him.

***

Tariq showered quickly, barely dried himself off and then sprayed deodorant all over. He slipped into his clothes and opened the door. He found himself in one of the Library's corridors, and it was empty. The lack of people, voices talking indistinctly, made that place much more different than he had ever seen. As he ran on the moving walkway, he realized that all the paintings and sculptures were gone. He then got to the door of The Librarian's office.

When Tariq entered, the chubby cat sleeping on a shelf raised his head and meowed.

The Library raised his glance from his satchel. "Hello, little man. You have been following me again, haven't you?"

Tariq looked away. "Yes."

"And what have I told you?"

"To make my own doors." Tariq gasped, looked at The Librarian with eyes agape. "I'm sorry, Mr. Librarian! I promise—"

"No matter. Tell me, what's it this time? Did your lockpick break again?"

"No, that's not it," said Tariq. He looked at the Librarian's satchel and tried to peek into it, but The Librarian closed it. Tariq smiled wryly. "Where are you going?"

"Certainly not in this universe. I have set camp here for quite a while, you know? Your universe sure is troublesome."

"But you can travel anywhere."

"Certainly. But I'm just one. I can't be everywhere at once. So it's better to have a base where people can come and ask for help. That's the best way to help them."

"Help them the same way you helped Anabia? And her parents?"

"Oh, so you met the girl. I gave her medicine, I do remember that. I just cannot forget that grumpy face."

"That's why I'm here. I don't know why, but she has the symptoms."

The Librarian shook his head. "Impossible. I cleared that plague."

"I saw it." Tariq felt the tears creeping down his cheeks. "Please, Librarian. I have money."

The Librarian lifted his palm. "Your money is of no interest to me," he said. "Alright. If it's to help someone else, I will give you more medicine." He turned around. "I think that I still have some on the top shelf…" He climbed on a gray ladder. "It's been a long of time since I—"

The shelf broke with a bang. Dust spread on the air and Tariq couldn't even see the man, but heard him coughing.

"Librarian! Are you all right?"

"Yes, yes…" He stepped down. "I'm not hurt. It's just that… dust…" He coughed. He covered his mouth with a kerchief; when he stopped coughing, he tried to hide it, but Tariq saw the blood.

"Librarian, you…" Tariq looked at the shelf: it had the same color as the furniture in Anabia's house. The dust in the air was also the same. "Are you okay?"

"Yes, yes. Don't mind." The Librarian placed the box with the medicine on the counter. "Here. No need to pay me."

Tariq picked up the box. "I have to go. I just realized something. Thank you, for everything."

"Don't mention it, little man."

"Are you sure you're alright?"

The Librarian rubbed his head. "Yes, nothing to worry about."

"Thank you. For everything."

Tariq turned around and ran. He didn't even get to see the big smile on The Librarian's face.

***

After coming back through the deactivated Library, the boat, the sewers, the airship and the grove, Tariq was back at Anabia's gray door. He didn't have a problem finding it; but, when he turned the knob and pushed, the door didn't move.

"Anabia!" he screamed, knocking hard. "Open up! I brought your medicine!"

"But it will get dark soon!" said Anabia's hoarse voice. "That's the hour the dragon! I'm not opening it!"

"There's nothing out here. It's just me!"

"You could be a dragon with Tariq's voice!"

Tariq's heart dropped and he began to gasp. This time, from anger.

"The dragon is inside your home!" Tariq screamed so hard that his throat hurt. There was silence; he just could hear his breathing. Then Tariq swallowed hard, said as gently as he could: "The structure of your house, your mobilia… everything's made of a material that's destroying you. People've been calling this the stone disease, because it creates things like stone-like inside of you that drain your life energy.

106

You don't have the plague; you're just digging your own grave."

Silence again.

After some time, Anabia answered: "You lie."

Tariq clenched his fist until it started trembling. He felt his bottom lip shivering and eyes tearing up, but he held it all in. *Seriously? After all I've been through?*

"Do whatever the hell you want," he said, turning around.

"Wait."

Tariq stopped.

"May I… May I ask you something?"

Tariq closed his eyes and sighed, said: "Go ahead."

"Why do you walk around opening doors?"

"Because I want to see what's on the other side."

"That's it?"

"That's it."

After one more moment of silence, Tariq continued: "If I see a door and feel like opening it, I'll open it. Because if I don't, I know I'll regret it for the rest of my life."

"But aren't you afraid?"

"Of course I am. I'm afraid that one day I'll open a door and see a monster… like a dragon." Tariq smiled. "And there's no fun if I always knew what was behind the doors, don't you think?"

"Did anything bad happen? When you were… exploring?"

"Of course! A lot of times! There was a time that a coven of witches left a lot of candy on their door, with a note that said 'there's more on the other side'. They almost boiled me alive."

Anabia began to laugh, then coughed. "You're so stupid! How could you enter a door like that?!"

"But I…"

She coughed hard.

"You need the medicine!"

"Leave it…" She coughed even more. "Leave it on the porch. I'll open it in the morning and pick it up with a broom."

"Anabia…" Tariq sighed. "Now it's my turn to ask a question: have you ever done something evil? Very, very evil?"

"No… I… I don't think so. I… No, I didn't! I'm sure of it. I've never done anything bad to anyone!"

"Then why are you so worried that evil is coming to knock at your door?"

Silence again. Tariq left the medicine on the floor. "The medicine is on the porch. There's food too. Pick it up… before it… rottens."

Tariq stared at that gray door for a while, hoping it would still open. But nothing happened. He wiped some tears off his face and turned around.

When he began walking on the grove, he heard a familiar sound. It was a sound that he knew so well: a key turning smoothly in the lock. And then, the squeak of a door opening slowly. It was music for his ears.

It took some time for Anabia to put her head out. She took several peeks first. After looking at all sides, as if waiting for an ambush, she left.

Tariq opened a smile when he saw her stepping out of her gray world and stepping on the colorful grove.

"So?" Tariq asked.

"It's… It's beautiful… I didn't know…"

"You can take the mask off, you know?"

Anabia stared at him without blinking, eyes agape.

"Go on," said Tariq. "Take that thing off. Breathe."

The girl undid the knot behind the head and took off the cloth. She closed her eyes and breathed, smiling. "It's so good…"

Tariq got closer. "Come on, there are a lot of things that I want to show you. There's a chocolate factory nearby. We can steal from it together."

When Tariq was going to hold Anabia's hand, the girl backed off.

"Wait," she said. "I… I get tired too easily. Just by walking a little I start panting!"

Tariq pressed his lips, shrugged. "I'll carry you."

"And my hair. It's getting so ugly…"

Tariq picked up the cloth and put it on Anabia's head—where headcloths should be. The girl smiled back. They held hands.

"Let's go. There are a lot of doors out there, and they're all just waiting to be opened. If there's no doors, we'll just make them."

The Egg
By Alex Evans

"My, my! Look at that lady under the potted palm. Her gold necklace must weigh at least a pound!"

"She's Tamora Caton, the wife of the director of the Institute of the Occult Sciences. I've heard the necklace is from Gandarah, like all the artifacts here."

"You think it's magic? Isn't it dangerous?"

"Oh, no! There is a Quorum man here to protect us."

"How do you know?"

"One of the Unicorn guards told me. There are always Quorum agents at exhibitions with magic things."

"You spoke to a Unicorn? Lucky girl! Which one?"

"The tall one with sandy hair, next to the statue of the Blind God. Isn't he handsome?"

The two barmaids were whispering with contained excitement while putting small hors d'oeuvres on a tray. As usual, they could not be bothered to include me in the conversation: after all, I was only an orphan girl from Gandarah. A halfwit. I had walked all the way from my native city to here when I was fifteen. Then, I had scrubbed floors, washed sheets and after years, I had progressed to being a barmaid for a fancy caterer.

I focused on filling the champagne glasses on the tray, trying not to stare at the display case three paces away. The one with the stone. A giant fire opal the size of two fists. A Mrs. Drake, some crazy collector, was paying us a thousand crowns to steal it. Drake was probably not her real name, but nor was mine. A thousand crowns were a fortune. My first heist. My hands were almost shaking with anticipation. I spilled a few drops of champagne and hastily dabbed them, but old Gerber had noticed.   Luckily, he could not guess the cause of my trouble. "I see those heathen statues make you nervous too." he commented.

"You have to live with your times!" chuckled Carley, wiping the counter. "Magic is the future! Soon, we will have magic factories, magic carriages… "

"Sure. All new and shiny…This is madness to pull things out of old tombs and come to look at them as if they were prized horses. And from Gandarah of all places!"

"Magic has returned and is here to stay, old man…"

The rest of the exchange faded at the back of my mind as Alb strode to the bar, an empty tray under his arm.

"Five minutes," he whispered.

I handed him another tray full of champagne glasses. He gave me a wink and wandered into the elegant crowd milling between the display cabinets. My eyes lingered on his broad shoulders until he disappeared behind a stuffed manticore. Alb. My love. I wondered what I would have done if he hadn't burst into my life three months ago. Died of boredom probably. Alb was everything I was not: handsome, fun, mysterious, his mind full of unexpected twists. He had turned my life into a whirlwind of romance and adventure. A dream from which I did not wish to wake up.

A mechanical organ played a bland and fashionable tune. The air resonated with the sounds of polite conversation. Elegant gentlemen and graceful ladies strolled between the urns, the sarcophagi and the display cases full of ancient artifacts, mostly jewels, caskets and vases. The opening night of the exhibition had attracted both the learned and the wealthy.

A Meralese gentleman with three diamonds embedded in his black forehead stopped at the bar and asked for a drink. I filled his glass with blue Cazalva wine, then glanced at the giant dragon eye clock. Four minutes. I took a deep breath and checked the tools in my pocket. With the money from that jewel, we would live like kings. No more patched up clothes, no more watery porridge. As a Gandaran, I knew I would never rise above a barmaid job, while I had ambitions and even dreams. Study. Travel… I addressed a short prayer to the Trickster whose granite statue was towering over the case. I didn't really believe in the Old Gods, but just in case.

I looked at Alb again across the hall. He was standing near the two Unicorn Company guards. He gave me a discreet smile. My heart leaped in my chest, and I looked away at the glass wall forming the western side of the hall. We were on the top floor of the ziggurat of the Institute of Occult Sciences, and through the glass, I had a spectacular view of the slate roofs below. A blue dirigible passed about fifty yards away, lazily overtaking a small airship as white as a cloud.

I patted my hair, wondering as usual if anyone had noticed it was dyed black. My heart was pounding and my mouth was dry, even though on the outside I was still the poised waitress. Part of the stress was the anticipation of what we were about to do. But another part was the *Power* from some exhibits getting on my nerves. I had never seen so much magic gathered in one place, even in my childhood among the smugglers and the ruin rats scouring the vestiges of Gandarah.

Power. Magic. This elusive energy flowed between several universes over a millennial cycle. After having left ours for almost four centuries, it had reappeared twenty years ago, bringing back fairies, elves and other creatures. I was among the rare unlucky ones who could perceive it and even use it… sometimes. Since my parents' death, nobody knew. People like me tended to vanish without a trace in the Quorum's laboratories.

Three minutes. Steady, Else. Steady.

A small group stopped in front of the bar to sample a few pastries. A Dagheri lady with colorless skin and tiny automatons studded with gems crawling through her blonde, curly hair. Her dress seemed to be made of sea foam and mist. She was accompanied by a large man with a walrus mustache and a younger one, with golden glasses perched on a hooked nose. His tie was made in an elaborate knot.

The woman said in a velvety voice: "I admire your courage, Mr. Marzel. You are doing your excavations in such difficult conditions!"

"You didn't have a problem with this new Gandaran nationalist group?" added the large man.

The woman flicked her clockwork fan. "Which group?"

The young scholar took a puff pastry topped with a tear of honey. "Just a few hot-headed young people who want to put our finds in a national museum."

"An interesting point of view," said the woman.

"Ridiculous. The notion of museum does not exist among these savages. No more than the idea of a national treasure. If any of these pieces were given to what serves them as government, it would immediately be sold under wraps. These items are much safer here!"

I sighed involuntarily, for they were speaking about my fellow countrymen. Myself, I had roamed the ruins of Gandarah with my father. Back then, I was a hungry and illiterate child. My small size allowed me to slip in the crevices and retrieve artifacts similar to those on display. We sold them for a pittance to amateurs like this archeologist.

A tall figure appeared behind the woman. A thin, dark man, as stiff as the Rod of Justice, dressed in a deep blue suit. He had given in to the new fashion without sideburns and was clean-shaven with only a thin black mustache. "Ah, Marzel, there you are! So, how many pieces here have been stolen from me?" he asked in a somewhat theatrical tone.

The archaeologist coughed, embarrassed. "None, Zoscan, I assure you."

"Liar! This morning I received a telegram from my partner: our guards caught one worker hiding a bracelet in his shirt. He readily admitted selling you the divination oware and even—"

He was cut off by a thunderous rumble at the other end of the hall. A thick cloud of smoke billowed above the sarcophagus adorned with lions. I heard someone scream:

"Fire!"

There was a moment of uncertainty. The three guests turned away from me. The two Unicorn guards walked towards the smoke. Its acrid smell wafted towards me. The other barmen wandered from behind the bar to take a closer look. I grasped the tools in my pocket.

Another piercing shriek rose at the other end of the hall. "The statue! There is smoke coming out of its mouth!"

Indeed, smoke was pouring from between the fangs of the Dragon Goddess. A lady fainted in a heap of pink silk. Guests crowded the door. Out of the corner of my eye, I saw Alb slipping towards me. Everyone had his eyes fixed on the other side of the hall. Everything was working according to plan. I edged towards the display case with the opal. In three minutes, the third smoke bomb would explode, engulfing the hall in thick fumes and setting the crowd into real panic. We would have a few minutes to break the glass and then run out with the guests.

I heard the two guards try to tell the crowd to leave the room in an orderly fashion, with "the ladies first." It had no effect.

"Now!" whispered Alb.

At that moment, a crash and a gunshot burst from the glass wall. The waltz played by the organ ended with a horrible squeal. The display case with the egg exploded into a thousand pieces, sending its contents to the floor. A strong smell of powder burned my nostrils. Half a dozen masked men burst out of the shattered window. Behind them swayed the little white aircraft I had spotted earlier. They spilled out into the room, brutally pushing or shooting those who stood in their way. Servants and guests collapsed. Blood spilled over the floor.

"Hands up, everyone! Now!"

The voice was young, masculine, with a strong Gandaran accent. The man pointed to the bar behind us. "All over there! Quick!" He punctuated his sentence with another shot, which shattered the mirror behind the bar. "Here's what happens when you steal Gandaran national treasures!"

I exchanged a glance with Alb: this was not in our plans! We followed the guests, walking on screeching glass. The wounded were wailing and moaning but no one dared to help them. Two thugs came to stand in front of us. Two others left the hall to watch the elevator and the stairs. The others began to smash the glass cases and grab their contents to transfer them into canvas bags. The smoke from our smoke bombs was escaping through the broken glass wall. Shots rang out from the stairs. No doubt, some guards had come to see what was going on. I noticed one of the men staring at me. I held my breath. Finally, he stepped closer and pointed his gun at me. "You! You're from Gandarah, aren't you? You serve those thieves!   Traitor! You come with us!"

Panic flooded my brain. I felt more than I saw Alb backing away from me. I was helpless... No. I had *Power*. But *Power* had a price. A day of my life for each spell, said my mother. But with those thugs, I would soon be dead anyway. I caught the magic wave with my mind and frantically wove a basic pattern around the statue of the Trickster. The same moment, our third smoke bomb went off from the crown of the Blind Goddess. My attacker turned away. The statue of the Trickster toppled over and fell, crushing him and taking along a few display cases. A thug panicked and fired at random. Seizing the chance, one of the Unicorn guards took cover behind a large urn and shot him. Two other guards came through the door, hid behind a sarcophagus and opened fire. One of the men standing guard near the aircraft toppled over. The pirates retaliated with a deafening noise. We all flattened ourselves on the floor. Bullets whistled over our heads. Smoke was slowly filling the place.

The man who seemed to be the leader grabbed one of the guests, an elderly gentleman, and pressed the barrel of his gun to his temple. The Unicorns stopped shooting.

"Let's go," the man yelped, jumping towards the airship.

They rushed into it and set off. More Unicorn guards burst into the room. Dazed, I lifted my head. And there, two feet away, covered in glass shards, lay the opal! I crept toward it and snatched it before slipping it into my apron pocket. Nobody paid attention. It was then I realized there was a wave of *Power* emanating from it, weak, but pulsating like the regular beat of a clock.

***

"We did it! My love, you're brilliant!"

I shook my head. Adrenaline flowed in my blood like champagne. "I didn't do anything special, just seized the opportunity. Nothing went as planned."

"Exactly! You seized the opportunity. Tomorrow, we will buy you the most beautiful dresses! And we'll have dinner at the Three Crowns, and the day after, we'll take the steamboat to Jarta first class. There, we'll live like king and queen! You'll see, it's a fabulous place."

It was well past midnight when we reached the Drake's Mansion. Waves of *Power* were rolling from it in rhythm, like the slow beats of a drum. I felt them from a good hundred paces away. I had never perceived anything like that. The banker must have been in possession of a very strong talisman, I thought. The rich and powerful loved them, even if they had no clue how to use them. Most of the artifacts were found without a user manual, and that was for the best.

Our visit was expected. As soon as Alb rang the bell, the door opened on a stately butler. He guided us through long, winding hallways decorated with exquisite works of art. I would have expected a hoard of flashy pieces in a banker's mansion, but this was something else. For what I knew, each one was unique. They came from the four corners of the world and even from the four corners of time. On a Triskelian cabinet stood a pale green Yartegian vase. On a modern secretary inlaid with mother-of-pearl chatted two Ranese antelope masks. Later, we passed a Dagheri landscape from the Late Expansion period, and on a lacquered table, a thousand-year-old Meralese shark made of jade was contemplating a sparkling modern cup. Moreover, each object was in perfect condition and highlighted by a daring harmony of shapes and colors. This mansion was a hoard of art.

I was already bewildered by the artifacts on display, but the magical vibrations disturbed me to a point of distraction. I wondered again what this talisman was. Finally, the butler opened a finely carved oak door and ushered us into a large study. Red velvet curtains hid the windows, and the walls were hung with golden silk. One of the walls was lined up with shelves full of books.   Facing the door, a tall woman in her fifties sat behind an ebony desk. Her iron gray hair was pulled back in an austere bun, and the collar of her deep blue gown was fastened with an agate brooch. Her long, slanted eyes were as green as the brightest emeralds. In her hand, she graciously held an amber cigarette holder with a cigarette on the end. As we entered, she raised it to her lips and let out a puff of smoke.

I could sense a slight hesitation in Alb, but he walked towards the desk with his usual swagger. I followed sheepishly.

"Good evening, ma'am."

"Good evening, Mr. Alb. I gather you have my opal?"

Her voice was a rich deep contralto. Alb gave me a nod.

"Of course, ma'am. There might be some glass on it. There were, um… unexpected complications."

I took the gem out of my stained apron. All the colors of the rainbow were playing on its smooth surface. It was incredibly beautiful. Almost hypnotic. Its *Power* was still pulsing with a steady beat. I put it on the desk before being totally enthralled.

"Good!" purred Mrs. Drake with another puff of smoke. She pulled a heavy envelope out of a drawer and handed it to Alb. He opened it. There were wads and wads of bills. I bit my tongue not to scream. I had never seen so much money. And it was ours! He slipped it into his jacket.

"Thank you, ma'am. It's a real pleasure to do business with you."

The woman smiled. "Likewise, young man."

Suddenly, I had the weird feeling that her teeth were a little sharper than those of a normal middle-aged woman. Another plume of smoke escaped from her mouth. And the realization hit me square in the chest. The *Power*. The mansion full of treasures. The teeth. The smoke.
She put down her cigarette holder.

"Now, if you will excuse us for a minute, Mr. Alb, there is a small matter I would like to discuss with your friend. Edward will show you to the parlor and bring you some refreshments.

I was too stunned to speak. Alb raised an eyebrow but dared not to argue. He turned around and headed for the door.

***

Once the door shut, Mrs. Drake grabbed the opal possessively and levelled her eyes on me before I could properly panic. "Please, take a seat."

I dropped mechanically on a mahogany chair. The wave of *Power* from the gem was almost drowned by the other one, but it seemed to me that the two were now pulsing in unison. She held up the opal in her hands. "Do you know what it is?"

I stared at it. Earlier, caught in the action, I did not have time to examine it carefully. Now... I strained my eyes. It was definitely not an opal. But it looked vaguely familiar. I had seen something like this a long time ago. When I had crawled into the ruins of the Academy of Magic Sciences in Gandarah.

Except then, it was not round. It was broken into several pieces and displayed on a shelf alongside a wyvern scale and a tangle of mermaid hair. Back then, I wondered how such a massive beast could be born out of such a small thing. "It's a dragon's egg… Your egg?"

The creature beamed. Her eyes appeared a little larger. Her teeth sharper. Smoke was constantly coming out of her mouth. "One of your mages stole it four hundred years ago, just before magic went away. I had to wait in Avalon until it returned. Luckily, humans do not know much about it anymore. No one recognized my egg for what it was. It should hatch in about forty years."

I nodded, completely bewildered. She carefully put it on her lap.

"Since you saved my child, I owe you a blood debt."

"You have already given the money to Alb, haven't you?"

"You are right, but it was not Alb who brought my egg. It was not him who took it. It was you. If the police had searched the two of you, you would have been the one to be arrested."

I frowned. "How do you know?"

"Because they told me."

"Who?"

"Let's say I like to hedge my bets. So, I sent you and those terrorists. One of you would have eventually brought my child back. And I put a spy among the guests to watch you all."

"These thugs killed quite a few people."

"Do you think I care? How many dragon eggs have your mages stolen in the name of their 'science'?"

I didn't answer. She let out another puff of smoke. "Anyway, you took all the risks."

"Of course. Alb and I are partners."

"Magic doesn't work that way. Did you tell him you had the *gift?*"

"No."

"Why?"

"I… I don't know."

She raised an eyebrow. "Oh, yes, you know. You are afraid that he might get scared and leave you."

I shrugged, trying to keep my composure. "If you like."

She nodded. "As I said, I owe you a blood debt.   Therefore, I will not pay you money. I will save your life."

 "By not telling anyone I have the *gift?*"

She clicked her tongue. "In the old days, before magic left, your kin used to say annoying a dragon was a bad idea. They also said that a dragon's advice was worth a thousand pounds of gold."

… And dragons never lie. I mentally finished the saying.   "All right. What is your advice, then?"

Her face turned serious. "Do not follow your friend tonight. He has no plan to share that money."

I shook my head in disbelief, but she continued. "He has already promised you to a man called Plumpy. Have you heard of him?"

Of course, who hadn't heard of Plumpy in the riverside slums? He owned the Parrot Cage, a luxury brothel for clients with "exotic tastes." When I had just arrived from Gandarah, one of his touts spotted me, or rather my Gandaran red hair, and offered to get me in. Since then, I'd been dying my hair black, to stay on the safe side.

"I can see on your face that you have heard of him," sighed Mrs. Drake. "Tomorrow evening, he will treat you to a fancy dinner at the Three Crowns. He will slip a drug into your food, and you will wake up locked in the Parrot Cage."

"How can you be so sure?" I stammered.

"You see, I hired Alb about three months ago. He told me he would find a way to be part of the catering team for this evening. However, since I did not entirely trust him, I made another man follow him. So, I know that three months ago, when your employer was appointed to cater for this evening, you met a dashing stranger and you asked your boss to hire him… Also, when the police will put together what had happened, they will know you were the person closest to the display case. They will look for you. Not Alb."

I gritted my teeth. That could not be! "Thank you for the advice."

"Unfortunately, that is not all. You have dropped a statue by magic. It could not have gone unnoticed by the Quorum agent. You might have seen her: a young Dagheri woman, her hair crawling with jeweled automatons. By now, she must be reporting to her superiors."

I closed my eyes. In my enthusiasm, I had forgotten the Quorum. Stupid, stupid, stupid. All my carefully rebuilt life. All my years of hard work. All my dreams. And Alb. No. Dragons never lie, but they can be wrong, just like everyone else.

"Come on, Miss Varil," whispered Mrs. Drake. "You have survived the civil war of Gandarah, the slums of this city and have so far succeded to escape the attention of the Quorum. You will manage."

She stroked her egg possessively. A few scales were starting to show on her cheeks. She pressed a button on her desk. The bookshelf swiveled, revealing a door. "Well, there's not much left to say. You can leave my office through there. Behind there is a hallway. At the end, you will come to a large circular room with a glass ceiling. On your right and on your left, there will be two corridors. The one on your right leads to the parlor where your friend awaits. The other leads to the servants' entrance. Whichever you choose, I wish you luck." Without a word, I stood up, nodded to Mrs. Drake and walked out like an automaton. I could feel tears pooling at the corners of my eyes. I followed the hallway, passing bronze statues, old paintings, and delicate porcelains, all blurred through the tears. I reached a beautiful circular room. The floor was covered in a sparkling mosaic depicting a dragon. Above my head, the stars glittered behind a glass ceiling. I stopped. Tears flooded my cheeks. Alb. His smile. His kisses. His laugh. His body against mine. His velvety voice in my ear. Even if he did not intend to sell me to Plumpy, would he stay with me if I was pursued by the Quorum? Could I ask that of him? Did he love me? I had put all my hopes on him. Not to be alone again. To have someone with whom to laugh and talk and live…

But the part of my brain which did my accounts, checked the inventory and prepared the bar, the part that had saved me from death, hunger, and my native city whispered: *You have just been kidding yourself, Else. All those years of loneliness had made you desperate. Why would a pretty boy fall in love with a plain girl from Gandarah? And when this thug threatened you tonight, where was he? Where were his sharp mind and his quick tongue? Of course, there was not much he could have done. But if Alb had had a gun pointed at him, wouldn't you have done something, anything, to protect him? No, my girl, when this guy called you up, you were on your own.*

I lowered my head and sobbed.

Then I turned left.

Beyond the Red Dunes

By Joachim Heijndermans

Banished! Forced to wander these sandy dunes till the end of his days, lest he made it to the other side and into Chu-thai. The rough sand had shredded the soles of his shoes, leaving his footwear little more than hats for the top of his feet. The last of his water swished back and forth in his bag, while his skin roasted to a red crisp under the unforgiving sun. Yes, the situation could not get any worse for Terryl.

"Sunny, innit?" his companion said with annoying cheer and a lively spring in his step. He rubbed the sweat on his bald head with his scarf, which made the shine from it even greater. His endless stamina and unfaltering cheer were infuriating. It seemed that, despite all odds, Terryl's punishment could get worse, as he was accompanied by the most annoying pain in his rear on the Myridion continent.

"I do love this desert. The awesome colors of the sand, highlighted under the contrast of the clear blue sky. Is there any other place on earth this magical? And that sun! Oh, blessed sun."

"Please don't…" Terryl grunted, preoccupied with not thinking about that blessed sun that burned his skin.

"Sunlight is good for you. Rejuvenates the soul. Life beams of fire, reigniting the heart. I love it."

"Please. I'm thirsty, nor am I in the mood to talk."

"Talking is good too. Keeps you focused. I figured you didn't want to walk in absolute silence."

Terryl rubbed the sweat from his eyes. "Actually, I was hoping I would," he muttered. When he opened his eyes again, the bald man's place was taken by a tall, dark-skinned woman dressed as a Q'all dancer.

"Why?" his companion asked, brushing her ebony hair out of her face. The bells on her ankles chimed as she walked. "Why are you so dour? It's a beautiful day, with not a cloud in the sky."

"Because I'm bloody miserable. I'm going to die in this horrible desert. I did nothing to deserve this horrible punishment." He turned his back, stomping off in a huff.

"I thought you stole gold from the duke?"

"I did no such thing!" he exclaimed. "It was his silver. And I did it for a good reason. To get away from a life of toiling in the smithy with not a Genny to show for it."

The woman had vanished. Terryl looked around until he caught the sight of a coarse-furred, one-eyed mongrel of a cat that had taken her place.

"Really?" his companion asked. "Are you certain that's the real reason?"

"Yes", Terryl sighed. "I had a perfectly good reason."

"I'm sure you did. Just like you had a good reason for stealing the girl's maidenhood.

"She lied. She threw herself at me, but I resisted her seductive wiles."

"Why?"

"Because I didn't want to get my cock lopped off as well as my hands!" he snapped, turning his back to the rugged tabby.

"Then why did she claim to her father that you did?"

"So he'd have my cock lobbed off! You can see why when given the choice of being unmanned, joining the army or walk the desert, I chose the desert."

A withered hand slowly patted Terryl on the back. The old man passed by him, having taken the place of the cat. "Oh, that I can see," his companion said as he leaned on his walking cane. "What I don't understand is why you decided to steal when you had comfortable employment with the blacksmith."

"Stealing is easier. And more fun." Terryl scoffed. "You speak as if you have never stolen anything yourself, Lifethief?"

"I've taken my share, I grant you. But it was what needed to be taken."

"Yeah, so you've said. You've still stolen more than I have. And of greater value too."

"So you are still upset about that?" his companion said. "Just leave me alone," Terryl moaned, walking a bit faster. But this was one companion who he could not avoid, no matter how hard he tried. In fact, his companion's speed increased. Terryl no longer saw the old man struggling to keep up, but an adolescent with pale, freckled skin, rushing past him up the dune.

"I can't. I'm headed the same way you are," his companion said, straightening her skirt and shaking the sand from her fire-red curls. "Like I said at the start: I'm seeing this walk through to the end."

Terryl sighed. His throat was as dry as the sand he walked on. He hated sand; long before he ever even set foot in the desolation of the northern desert. It was coarse, hot and empty. The perfect place to send people to die of thirst or boredom.

"Yow!" he suddenly screamed out. He felt a sharp pain stinging him in his large toe. His heart nearly stopped when he saw what had plunged its razor-like fangs into his skin. "A snake! I've been bit!"

"So you have," his companion said. "But you should be relieved to hear it's not a snake. It's a worm, and at this size, it's harmless."

"I don't care what it is! Get it off! Kill it!"

"Why? It's not its time. Must this little worm die because you couldn't watch your step?"

"Please! I'll die!"

"Neither of you will. But if it distresses you so——" his companion sighed. She took the head of the worm between her decorated fingers and gently squeezed it. It let go without struggle, before being dropped. Within seconds, it vanished, burrowing into the red sand. "Is that better?" she asked.

Terryl wept. He pressed his face against his arms. "I hate everything about this place. Why me? Why did it have to be me?"

"Well, you're a thief who entered the duke's castle, stole his daughter's silver gown and then attempted to blame it on the blacksmith. All things considering, you got off easy with banishment."

Terryl laughed bitterly. "You're right. All I need to do is cross into Chu-thai without dying. Not a problem."

"One snag in your plan," his companion said, brushing his brown hair out of his eyes as he looked to the sun. "You're heading for Chu-thai, right?"

"Yes?"

"Chu-thai is north. You've been walking west for three days."

At that point, a scream of pure rage and exhaustion was heard across the red wastes, with only a startled red worm to hear it.

***

Sand dunes on one end, and sand dunes in the other. Nothing but an endless sea of red sand. It was all he'd seen since his banishment began.

"Just how vast is this desert?" Terryl asked.

"Why do you ask?"

"I want to know how much further I have to walk before I reach the end," he said, with a destitute tone lingering on his every word.

"Have you been keeping count of your steps?" his companion asked, stroking her hands over her dark ebony breasts. While she was alluring, Terryl focused on his question.

"No. Have you?"

The companion hesitated. "Yes, I have. And you have much further to walk."

"Will we reach Chu-thai before I drop dead?"

"We could, but Chu-thai is not the first place you'll find once we pass beyond the dunes.

"Damn," Terryl grunted. "What is?"

"Mountains. And hills. And firewyrms."

"There are no firewyrms," he scoffed.

Once again, although his attention had been diverted for but the briefest of moments, Terryl lost sight of his tanned, nude temptress of a companion. He was startled when a blonde child ran through his legs, nearly causing him to fall over.

"But there are wyrms. I guarantee it," his companion giggled, as she jumped around.

Terryl chuckled. "Why do they call them worms? If the stories are true, they're much larger than little worms."

"Have you seen a firewyrm?"

"No. But I heard they're the size of a battleship." His companion leaped toward him. Where once was a small round face was now a beak attached to a black head of a raven. It ruffled its wings, pecking ticks from its feathers. "They were."

"Yeah. Suppose they're dead then?"

"No. They're just not as large anymore."

"How would you know?"

"I just know," his companion said, as he heaved his knapsack over his broad shoulders. The sun was reflected off his brown, oiled skin. Terryl caught himself eyeing this new incarnation of his companion a bit longer than he'd done before.

They walked on. The air seemed to get thicker. Terryl daren't look up, fearing the sun would scorch his eyes. His long hair roasted his scalp. Droplets of sweat lingered on his lips, leaving a salty taste that further aggravated his thirst.

"Come now, let's amuse ourselves!" his companion suggested.

Terryl sighed. "And what would you have us do, oh unswayed one? Sing songs? Do a little dance? Make a bit of love?" he said, with a twinge of hope in his voice. But his desire faded when he couldn't find the well-toned man. The small gryphon had taken his place.

"Let's play a game!" she chirped, leaping onto his shoulder, shaking her brown mane and folding her purple wings in. Her claws dug into his skin, causing Terryl to wince. "Do you know 'Told to behold'?" she asked.

"Of course. I used to play it with…friends," he answered.

He tried to ignore the pain, clenching his eyes shut. But once he opened them, he felt warm fingers glide over his neck. The young man's golden eyes made Terryl's heart skip a beat.

"I will begin," his companion said. His thin, slender hands grazed his buttocks, revealing his diamond teeth in a broad grin. Terryl gulped, taken aback by his beauty. "You will be told, what I am to behold; something that is…blue."

Terryl sighed. "The sky," he said.

"Correct! Your turn."

"Must I?" he groaned.

"Yes," said his companion. "Don't be a marplot."

He relented. "You will be told, what I am to behold; something that is…red."

"The sand!" his companion said cheerfully. When Terryl confirmed she was correct, she twirled with joy. "My turn!

You will be told, what I am to behold; something that is…red!"

"I just gave you sand," Terryl protested.

"It's not the sand," his companion said with a smirk. "But it is close to your feet."

Terryl looked down. To his horror, he saw another worm inching its way towards his nearly bare feet. In a panic, Terryl leaped into the air. He danced around the little worm, whose white teeth were primed to bite. In a moment of blind fear and fury, Terryl brought his foot down, crushing the worm. Blood and entrails stuck to his foot, a sensation that horrified him.

"Hmn," his companion muttered. "I suppose it was more of a dark orange; your foot is definitely redder. Also, are you going to eat that?"

Terryl shook his head, flicking the worm's remains from his foot. His companion leaped at them, happily chowing down on the meager meal it. Terryl watched the black hound eat the bloody remains, wagging its tail with joy.

"So no lecture on how it wasn't its time to die?" Terryl scoffed.

"No, it was its time," his companion said, lapping the blood from its face. His companion looked him in the eye. Terryl recognized these eyes as the true eyes of the stranger. The same eyes he saw as a boy. "There are three that I must take," said the companion. "This was the first. There are two more. By accompanying you, I will take what I must."

For a moment, Terryl felt cold. The way his companion looked at him with icy eyes. A memory returned. That night, his mother on the bed breathing her last, and the third entity standing within the shadows. A promise was made. Would it be fulfilled soon?

***

Terryl slumped over, exhausted, but still angry enough to curse.

"Are you all right?" his companion asked, while she cleaned her ears out with her long, purple tongue.

"No, I'm not all right," he muttered. "I hate it here." Terryl turned around, racing towards his companion and flailing his hands wildly. "Why are you here? What do you want from me? Damn your eyes!"

"I told you," his companion replied. "I'm going the same way as you are."

His companion inhaled deeply. He crossed his large arms, contemplating Terryl's question. "The reason is twofold, actually," his companion said. "One, I need to be where your journey ends."

"And the second?" he asked.

His companion pointed his finger toward the horizon. His lips twitched excitedly. Terryl had never seen his companion so thrilled by looking at nothing at all. This further weirdness did not surprise him, as the companion had displayed many odd qualities. Then he saw it. In the distance, emerging from beneath the sand. A red shape taking to the air.

"Is...is that—?"

"Be silent, Terryl the thief," his companion hissed. "You might be the first of your kind to see this firsthand."

With the sun blinding him, Terryl barely made it out. But once he could, he couldn't believe his eyes. It was a slender creature, no bigger than a hound, flying without the use of wings.

"A firewyrm! They're actually real!"

"Indeed they are," his companion concurred.

The wyrm danced gracefully through the air. Its long flowing manes seemed to change color as it fluttered in the wind. What surprised Terryl was that the creature didn't roar; he always assumed they would. But no, this beast howled in a pattern. A sad to the melody of three short yelps, followed by a deep long bellow.

"What is it doing?" Terryl asked. "Is it in pain?"

"No, it's a mating dance."

"A mating dance? But it's alone."

"No," his companion said. "It's not." Terryl turned around, startled by her height and eight eyes, as dark as the night. The frills around her neck and head rose up, as she spread her four wings and leaped into the air.

Before he could realize what his companion's cryptic answer meant, the sand beneath his feet began to move. The earth rose and heaved him into the air. Terryl hollered as he fell; his impact broken by the sand. A warm gale blew him further across the dunes. He regained his footing and turned around, coming face to face with a row of white razors. The teeth of a firewyrm, which rose from beneath the dunes and took to the air. Sand rained down on Terryl, as the beast flew up towards its mate. This one was as large as a horse, yet this made it no less intimidating. The gleam from its golden scales blinded him briefly. Terryl was mesmerized by the riches encased in the hide of this magnificent wyrm. He doubted the wealthiest man in Myridion had that much gold.

The beast circled in the air, listening to the howls of the other wyrm. It twirled along with the music that was the resonating moans of its potential mate. Both creatures were locked in a majestic dance, circling through the air at a gentle pace, inching closer to one another. When the smaller one wrapped its body and teeth around the other, Terryl knew the mate had been accepted.

Knowing what came next would be messy, Terryl walked away. But it was the sudden bloodcurdling scream that alerted him just in time to dodge the large splatter of blood falling from above. Another followed, along with a hunk of dark red meat and golden scales. Above, the larger of the two beasts dug her teeth into the smaller. She tore her mate to bits whilst still breeding with him, his hemipenis still locked onto her body. The female then opened her maw and unleashed an inferno into the smaller's body. His shriek was hell to Terryl's ears. He wriggled and sputtered as his flesh charred until the female pried herself loose and dropped her mate. A wave of sand shot into the air as the disemboweled remains of the smaller firewyrm hit the soil. The female took flight, ascending further into the air. Despite his best instincts, Terryl had to take a closer look. What happened for her to turn against her mate so suddenly?

When he neared the remains of the younger one, he was thrown to his back by a massive fireball. Small bursts of fire ruptured out from the smoldering remains of this once-mighty creature. Standing next to the head of the dying wyrm stood his companion. No longer the blue nymph, he now was even taller, with curved horns on his head nestling a crown of flames. With the claws of his blackened hand, he carved a symbol into the beast's flesh.   The wyrm's breathing was erratic, hampered by the wounds in the creature's neck. The life was leaking out of its throat in the form of flames and blood. His companion spread his leathery wings wide, and dug his claws into the beast's hide. With a swift motion, he twisted the creature's neck. The cracking sound was loud and brutal. His companion turned to face him. "Two down. One remains," he said. Terryl gulped, feeling as if a dark haze had shrouded them both when his companion looked at him.

"Why?" Terryl asked. "Why did she do that?"

"It is their way. When the dance reaches its climax, the singer of songs dies, while the mother lives on to bear her children," he said, his four eyes glowing a frightening shade of yellow. "She will take her leave, and scatter her eggs across the dunes."

"It's…it's so cruel." The smoke smoldering from the carcass stung his eyes. When he wiped them, he was greeted with the more pleasing visage of an aged beauty, her silver hair adorned with sapphires.

"Not really," his companion said, stepping carefully to avoid staining her pink dress with wyrm blood. "It's just their way."

"Do all wyrms mate like this?"

She shrugged. "I don't really know much about making life."

Like his companion predicted, the female flew off. As sudden as she had appeared, she vanished on the horizon. Scattered in the sand lay wyrm scales, their gold shine reflecting sunlight. Never one to miss an opportunity, Terryl began collecting scales and loading them into his satchel. To make space, he threw his knife away.

"What are you doing?" his companion asked.

"What does it look like? These are firewyrm scales. One of these could go for a thousand Gennies on the Ellecome markets. Imagine what I could get for a bag full of them in Chu-thai? I'll be rich!"

"You're still fixated on obtaining wealth? Even after it landed you in this predicament?"

"I had a good reason for stealing that silver!"

His companion said nothing, simply staring at him. Terryl hated the way those eyes judged him. "It's fascinating you feel that becoming a wealthy man is worth desecrating the corpse of this great wyrm."

"No-one will take offense to it out here. I'll be rich, I tell you."

"And what good would that wealth do you?"

"It'll buy me a house to shield me from the cold," Terryl laughed. "If I get sick, I can buy medicines. With this, I will never be afraid again. I will never die."

"Never die?"

"Rich men never die. It's a fact. You've seen the old bastards. Their long grey beards and fat bellies."

"So you steal to live forever?"

"Trust me. With this, I will never die!"

His companion's eyes gleamed again, bemused by how wrong the thief truly was.

***

Terryl's pace had slowed down considerably. The additional weight in his pouch had taken its toll. When his trek across the red dunes began, Terryl never imagined he could feel any more miserable. He was wrong. Walking underneath the blazing sun with a sack filled with wyrm scales was much, much worse.

He discarded his emptied water skin. It was dead weight anyway. Where he was going, he could buy as much water as he wanted. He was going to buy a well. And a house. And maybe get a wife. He could buy anything.

He groaned. The weight strained his back. How were the scales so heavy? Wyrms fly! How could heavy beasts soar into the sky so easily? "How much further?" Terryl asked his companion.

"Much, much further," he replied, shaking his fat belly as he laughed. He stroked his fingers through his thick white beard, as the bell on his hat chimed. "We have yet to reach the foot of the red mountains."

"And beyond that, is Chu-thai?"

"Oh yes. You only need to scale the red cliffs."

Terryl groaned. The thought of climbing the mountainsides with his heavy sack was too much.

"Can you wait? I…I need to lighten my load. Leave something behind."

"Leave what? Your water skin is gone. As is your knife," his companion said. Terryl hated to see him grinning so smugly.

"You laugh," Terryl snapped. "But I will leave enough to pay my way. Just a few of these will still leave me a rich man. Yes! Rich! Never die!"

"I said nothing," his companion laughed. "And I don't doubt your upcoming wealth. I just worry about your safety."

"Oh? And pray tell, what could jeopardize my safety more than this desert?"

"The wyrms in the mountains. Many, many wyrms." Terryl shrugged his shoulders, biting through the pain of his sack's strap digging into his skin. "Wyrms?"

"They happen to be easily agitated. Especially to those who commit crimes."

"What offense could my theft of the silver gown cause to wyrms?"

His companion smirked. She shook her head. Her eyebrow, decorated with rings, raised. It was then he realized that she wasn't looking at him, but rather the heavy satchel on his back. She mimed with her hands the motion of a fireball, an illusion that was further helped by her cinnabar-colored nails. Terryl, now the thief of wyrm scales, gulped.

"Bugger this! Damn it all!" he shouted, heaving the heavy sack away. It hit the sand with a loud 'dud'. The impact startled a small worm that had been resting underneath the hot sand. It scurried off and, to Terryl's surprise, leaped into the air and flew toward the horizon. He tried to follow the little creature as it fluttered through the air, but a vastly more interesting sight caught his eye instead. Still far beyond his reach, but there they were; the mountains. The end of the desert!

"Do you see that?" he asked. "Please tell me I haven't gone mad."

The woman was gone. Terryl found his companion, now a dark stag beetle, sitting on his shoulder. "I see them," said his companion, slowly clicking its mandibles.

"How much further are they? Can we reach them?"
"We can. In two days' time."
Terryl shuddered. Two more days of this impossible heat, with freezing cold to nearly strangle the life from him each night "Well, regardless, it is an end to all this desert."

"Whoever said anything about no more desert?"

"You said that the desert ends when we meet the foot of the Chu-thai mountains!"

"Oh yes. The Myridion desert ends with the mountains. Then there are the wyrm mountains. And then there is the Chu-thai desert."

An expletive could be heard across the sandy dunes, to which only a small little worm reacted to with confusion.

***

Terryl laid on his back. The sun was setting, both on the distant horizon and himself. For once the sand felt cool against his skin. His companion hovered around him, doing nothing in particular. He licked his dark fur. She combed her red hair. It writhed its slender body in the sand. Soon enough, his companion did nothing at all, save for wait at his side.

"I'm dying, aren't I?" he asked.

"Yes," said his companion. "You have not had water. You will die before sunrise without it."

"It wasn't meant to end like this," he cried, but the tears did not come. He had no drop of water to spare in him. He was spent. "I wanted a house and riches and…someone. I didn't want to end up here."

"Very few are pleased where their roads lead them," his companion sighed. "If you could, would you live your life differently?"

Terryl shook his head. "No. I could lie, but I know I'd still have been a thief. I might have reconsidered stealing the duke's daughter's gown."

"Or her maidenhood?"

"I didn't steal that. I would never."

"I believe you."

"I've never even been with a woman. I—"

"I know."

Terryl looked to the night's sky. He tried to count the stars, but in his state, he barely came to ten. His companion knelt beside him.

"Do you steal because of me?"

"What do you mean?" Terryl asked.

"I took your mother those many years ago. I could see how a boy that young would think wealth could chase the blight from her. But all the gold in the city could not have cured her illness. She was mine to take."

"If we had money, she would've never gotten sick to start with," Terryl grunted.

"Perhaps. But it was never the contents of her purse that led me to take her."

Terryl's voice cracked. "After you took Mem, I swore you'd never get me. I'd be rich and eat well and live forever. I'd swim in gold, no matter how I got it."

"You know it wouldn't have mattered, don't you?"

"I do," Terryl laughed dryly. "But you try to convince a six-year-old cast out into the streets, watching the rich men walk past as his Mem rots in the earth."

A wispy sound escaped the companion's mouth, a pale imitation of a sigh. "Then I'm sorry for setting on this path of thievery. I make it a point to stay out of the affairs of those I have yet to take. But the young tend to catch glimpses of me. It changes them. For that, I apologize."

"Don't be. It was my choice. I was so frightened by you, so I chose poorly," Terryl laughed dryly. "It's funny, though."

"What is?"

"You apologized. I never imagined you even could."

"Neither did I," said the figure. Terryl looked at his companion. Either it was his thirst or the burning sun that muddled his vision, or his companion seemed to lose all semblance of shape.

"You look different," he said.

"Don't I always?" asked the companion.

"Yes. I suppose you do," he said, chuckling dryly. "Can you hold my hand?"

"No. I cannot."

"Why? Isn't that what you do? Isn't that why you were following me?"

"Would you come with me?" his companion asked.

"I would. I think I was ready when we began. I just hadn't realized."

"Your kind usually don't."

Terryl coughed. He knew that the moment he closed his eyes, Death would take him along. He wondered who was truly following whom. Whatever the case, he was ready to go. To walk into the dark beyond where only the iron-vultures venture, and become one with the mist. Would Bryant, his first love, be there? Or his Mem? Could he face her, knowing how he used her death to excuse his actions? He hoped she would be, if not for the absolution, then just to feel her arms around him once more. He was ready.

Then, high above them, a shriek. With a loud thud, a plump fat bird with orange feathers dropped from the sky. It sputtered around, its throat speared by an arrow. Terryl's companion approached the wounded animal, crouched down and stroked its head with hazy fingers. The throttles stopped. It was dead.

"My journey has come to a close for now. Take heed of yourself, Terryl the thief. 'Till we meet again."

And with that, his companion was gone. Terryl was alone, yet less afraid than he would have imagined himself to be. In the distance, he heard voices. A young boy, a bow strapped across his back, stood over him. He yelled out in words unknown to Terryl. An old man and a young girl joined them, astonished to find someone in these mountains. The old man retrieved his water skin and pressed it against Terryl's lips. The cool liquid stung his blistered skin, but he welcomed it. The girl pulled a strip of dried meat from her pouch and pushed it into his mouth, which he chewed with great effort.

The three lifted his body up and moved him. Carried over the rocky terrain by his saviors, Terryl felt he would live. He would be nursed back to his former strength. He would live a simple life. Perhaps he would finally get that house. Perhaps marry. Live a simple life. A good life.

But he knew that for the rest of his life, he'd be waiting. There would be a day that his companion would return to take him on another journey. And once again, they would walk together toward a place unknown.

The House-Berg on the Lake

By Ismail Ahmad

Hank squelched his way over the hard snow, his two miserable pieces of catch dangling from his belt. Six hours out on the freezing lake, and this was all he had to show for it, a pair of miniscule fish that couldn't feed a mouse. He'd dropped his best rod into the water, slipped into the hole whilst trying to retrieve it, and then soaked his already numb feet. Now, all he wanted to do was get home so he could sulk in his bed in peace.

Soon, he came to the line of wooden markers sticking in the snow, which he used to mark the trail to his house. Then the battered porch of his house came into view. Its walls had enough splinters to skewer an army, its windows were thinner than a damp piece of paper, and the door could barely protect the inside from a light breeze. But it was home, and it was just where Hank wanted to–

There was a dragon on the roof.

The horse-shaped head of the great beast was at least as long as Hank. Her eyes glowed a dull red, contrasting heavily with her smoky grey skin. Her tail, almost as long as her body, wrapped around the rear gutter, before making its way back to rest its tip beside her head. Razor sharp black claws gleaned, even in the pale sunlight, and on her back a pair of leathery wings rested folded up on her thick, scaly back. The creature's enormous shape completely covered the thatched roof of the house – how she had not fallen through was anyone's guess.

Hank stared up into the dragon's ember-red eyes, unsure whether to be amazed, shocked, or horrified. He decided to settle on annoyance.

He pointed and said to the dragon, "Excuse me, that's my house."

There was a short pause.

"So?" she said.

"So, I'd like you to get off."

"Or what?" The dragon didn't sound angry. Just mildly irritated.

Hank put two fingers to his lips and gave a loud whistle. "Here Grover, come Grover, come boy! Atta boy, atta boy, come out to me!"

The door creaked open. An ancient bloodhound, with a nose droopier than a dying willow tree, trudged out. Its hair was thin and patchy, its legs shook as it plodded over the frozen floor of the porch, and its eyes strained to stay open in the harsh winds of the tundra. It really was the most pitiful dog one could imagine.

Hank pointed at the dragon and called again. "Come on Grover, chase the dragon, if you do, I've got some lovely fish for supper!"

Grover languidly turned his droopy head to look at the (rather amused) dragon. After several seconds, he gave a loud sigh, and dropped to the ground. He then began to snore.

Cursing, Hank threw down his puny fish, and stomped over to Grover, giving him a nudge with his boot. "Oi, get up! Useless arse! What do I keep you around for, eh?"
There was a sound like charcoal being shaken with a shovel. Hank listened and noticed that it was coming from above him. The dragon – she was chuckling at him!
"Leave him. The poor thing couldn't catch a snail!" she said.

Gritting his teeth, Hank turned and shook his fist at the great lizard.

"Maybe first leave my house! At least Grover never kicked me out of my own home!"

"I didn't kick you out of your own home," said the dragon curtly, "I am merely resting on top of it. You are free to enter and exit your abode as you pl–"
There was a sudden bright glow in the dragon's eyes. Her jaws opened wide enough to swallow a man whole, showcasing lines of razor-sharp teeth. There was a sound like a blizzard being drowned, interrupted by a ball of black blood being expelled down the trail Hank had just come down. The dragon coughed and coughed again, each round deafening the landscape around it, whilst painting it black. Finally, she ceased her coughing fit, resting her head wretchedly on her claws. A mild groan escaped from her lips.

Hank peered out from behind the snow mound he had taken cover behind. He began to edge his way over to the dragon, pausing only to trip over the immobile shape of Grover (who had slept through the entire thing).

Hank picked himself up and glanced at the dragon. The dragon gazed back.

"Are you alright…?" asked Hank feebly.

The dragon grunted. "Did that sound alright to you?" she grumbled.

"Sorry." said Hank. He shuffled his feet, unsure of what else to say.

"Okay," he said at last, "You can stay."

The dragon's lips curled at the ends in a reptilian smile. "Thank you." she said.

Hank sighed and stooped down to Grover. After much struggling and cursing, he managed to wake the old hound, and make him go back into the house on his own. He took one last look at the unwell monster lying on his rooftop and shut the door.

***

Night fell. The stars gleamed like snowflakes suspended in time. The Moon was a luminous orb in the sky, its light glittering off the endless snowy fields. The air was still and silent.

The dragon still rested on top of the house, her eyes fluttering up and down rapidly. She felt tired, but try as she might, she just couldn't get to sleep. As the Sun had gone in, she really began to feel the cold through her thick scales. The thatched roof was warm, but the house was out in the open, with no cover.

She heard the sound of the door opening and glanced down. Below was the figure of Hank, huddled under a thick, fur coat. He had two steaming mugs in his hands.

Hank gingerly raised one of the mugs. "Do dragons drink tea?"

The dragon smiled. "Yes," she said, "However, if I tried to take it from such a small mug, I most likely would break it. But thank you."

Hank shrugged and took a sip. He turned to the drying blood which still stained the snow along the trail.

"Ate something bad, did you?" he asked.

The dragon grunted. "As it so happens, I did." she said.

"What did you eat?"

"A troll."

"A troll?" Hank screwed his face up in disgust. "Why would anyone want to eat a troll?"

"Because he was making fun of me."

"I see." Hank looked back at the dragon. "Very reasonable response."

"As it turned out, that was not the case."

The two remained in silence, gazing at the Moon. Then the dragon spoke.

"I'm sure fish taste better than troll," she said, nodding to Hank's catch lying in the snow, "Yet you have not laid a finger on yours."

Hank shrugged. "Might as well eat air for all the good they would do. Not been much good fishing as of late."

"Why ever not?"

"Dunno. And there ain't much else to eat around here. I have some food stored, but it ain't enough for all winter."

"I see. A great shame. I know of a good place for catching fish, but it is much too far for a person to walk."

"I see." said Hank. He glanced up at the dragon with a bright light in his eyes. "But maybe not so far for a dragon to fly–"

"Absolutely not!" said the dragon abruptly. "Besides, even if I were the type to allow men to ride my shoulders like a common mule, there would still be a problem."

The dragon then raised one of its great arms, showing a ragged leathery wing beneath. Hank gasped. The wing had been torn like the sails of a shipwreck. A massive hole had punctured it, leaving the surrounding skin to hang limply around it.

"Was that the troll?" Hank exclaimed.

The dragon nodded. It lowered its wing.

"Do not fret," she said. "It will heal in time. If I have not starved to death beforehand."

Hank sat down on the snow. He felt quite shaken by the sight of the mutilated wing.

"Well, where is this great fishing place you talked about." he asked.

The dragon nodded in the direction of the Moon. "Five leagues yonder." she said. "A region of the lake near the Marblellous Mountains."

"You mean marvellous."

"Marblellous," emphasized the dragon. "They were named by geologists."

"Oh."

He gazed in the direction that the dragon had nodded to. "Can't walk there, can't fly there. And the ice is too thick to boat across."

"Not a problem for me," said the dragon, swishing the tip of her tail, "I'm not as strong as I was, but I could still probably crack the ice."

"Okay, but then what? Swimming there is out of the option for me in these frigid waters, and in your condition, I doubt you could do it. And as for boats, all I've got is tiny rowing boat, too small for you, and too difficult for me to row five leagues within a reasonable amount of time."

"True," sighed the dragon, "If only we could both bring the house with us."

Hank nodded and put his head in his hands. Then suddenly, he sprang up. He looked at the dragon with excitement in his eyes.

"That's it!" he exclaimed.

"That's what?" said the dragon, with a confused expression on her face.

"We'll just take the house with us!" cried Hank.
The dragon's expression flickered between mirth and concern. "And how would we do that, strange human?" she queried.

"Well, you can crack the ice with your tail, right?" said Hank, his voice rising with excitement, "If you can crack a piece of ice large enough to fit the house, and then help me push it onto the ice, we'll have our own personal iceberg/boat. Then, we can take it in turns to paddle, you with your claws, and me with one of those large wooden markers along the trail! It'll be easy!"

There was a brief silence. Then there was a burst of sound as though a hundred barrels of gunpowder were exploding. The dragon's mouth was open as she shook with laughter.

"You really are a strange human," she exclaimed, "Really, as if such an idea would work!"

"Well, do you have a better one then?" asked Hank. "Eventually we're gonna starve out here. What do we have to lose if it doesn't work out?"

The dragon sighed, "Even if I were to entertain the possibility of this working," she said, "How would I push the house onto the ice without breaking it down?"

"This house is just a box of wood." said Hank, "There are no foundations in the ground; with enough force, it should move."

The dragon sighed again. She looked all around the white, wind-swept tundra. Then she turned in the direction of the Moon, where far off lay the Marblellous Mountains. She gently raised herself onto her mighty yet shaky legs, and half-leapt, half-fell into a snow heap at the side of the house. She clambered out, her great height towering over Hank, with her head peering over the roof of the house.

"Ingrid." said the dragon.

Hank grinned. "Hank." he replied.

Ingrid smiled. "Show me what to do." she said.

***

153

First, with a little help from Hank, and no help from Grover, Ingrid used her great bulk to push the shabby house a little way onto the lake. She was surprisingly gentle, pausing now and then to make sure her incredible strength didn't overwhelm the frail beams and boards of Hank's glorified shack.

Then, after Hank had grabbed a few of the wooden markers from the trail, Ingrid began to smash the ice around the house with her enormous tail. Each swing crashed into the ice with an earth-shattering sound, sending small pieces of ice flying hundreds of yards away.

Hank meanwhile was using some thick pieces of twine to tie several markers together to form one long pole.   Grover had at this point awoken with all the commotion and noise and had decided to give Hank a hand. His saliva provided some extra adhesive to keep the twine tied together.

Soon, the party were ready. Standing in position around their new floating home (which Hank had tentatively named the House-Berg). Ingrid stood on top of the house, peering around the lake. Around the house was at least five yards of ice, giving Hank and Grover enough room to roam around. The icy blanket over the lake was cracked up into ice floes which bobbed back and forth, and side to side, making loud clunks as they knocked into each other.

Hank was looking at these floes with a pained expression on his face. He hadn't thought of them. While the ice sheet was broken up, the floating ice was still in the way, preventing the House-Berg from moving forward. He looked up at Ingrid.

"I don't suppose you could also sink some of those pieces of ice in front of us, could you?" he asked in his politest voice.

Ingrid stared at him for a bit. Then she smiled.

"Stand back," she said, "I have a better idea."

Hank and Grover retreated to beneath the front porch, as the dragon above them extended her long neck over the roof. They heard her inhale so deeply that their ears popped. There was a load roar and the world ignited!

White hot flames blew furiously over the icy landscape. Steam erupted from the snow, tendrils reaching out desperately for the stars and Moon. Hank covered his eyes and Grover buried his face, as the light and heat attacked them with matchless intensity. Finally, after what felt like hours, Ingrid closed her jaws and the world returned to normal. Only this time, there was a clear path of water waving straight in front of the House-Berg, ice floes bobbing to its sides as though afraid of a second burst of flame from the almighty dragon.

Hank waved to Ingrid. "That was amazing!" he cried.

Ingrid smiled. "Oh, it was nothing really," she said, not too modestly.

Without another second to lose, Hank grabbed his makeshift oar and ran to the front right-hand side of the House-Berg. He took a deep breath, shoved almost the entire oar into the water, and pushed with all the strength tea and an empty stomach could give him.

The House-Berg rocked from side to side while jerking forwards a few inches. Again, Hank pushed with the oar, trying to build momentum, but it did not seem to be enough to move the House-Berg more than a few more inches at a time.

"Let me try on the other side," he heard Ingrid call. There was a rustling and huge splash, followed by a girlish squeal. The House-Berg rocked even more, making Hank slip onto his face.

"What happened?!" he called.

Ingrid lifted the tip of her tail to show him. It was wet and shivered like a frightened snake. "Cold." She giggled. However, Ingrid's tail and Hank's oar together proved enough to slowly move the House-Berg down the melted path that Ingrid had made. As they drifted along, Hank chuckled aloud, while Ingrid grinned widely, her rows of white teeth gleaming in the moonlight (Hank was very glad that she was too full of troll to think about food for a while).

Soon, they managed to get a rhythm going. Ingrid would melt a path with her scorching flames, one that stretched for about a quarter of a mile. Then, with her tail and his oar, Ingrid and Hank would row down the watery path. When they came to the end of a path, Ingrid would call for Hank and Grover to take cover, and she would melt a new course for them.

***

After what felt like forever, the trio arrived in the middle of the lake, where the ice had thinned out, and Ingrid didn't have to use her flames anymore. Meanwhile, Hank had stripped to his vest, oaring being sweaty work even in such frigid temperatures. He was able to row the whole House-Berg now that they had enough momentum with no ice floes providing resistance against the sides. This allowed Ingrid's tail to take a rest. She was warming its tip in her mouth.

The stars had gone out completely. The Moon had sunk long ago. Darkness enveloped the House-Berg completely. Only the dull red eyes of Ingrid provided any source of light for its peculiar inhabitants.

Then, a spark of light appeared on the horizon. The dull yellow of dawn faintly signalled the break of a new day. Several humungous shapes miles high prevented all but a sliver of daybreak from being seen by the House-Berg's residents…

Just then, Grover, who had been resting by Hank's feet, perked up. The old dog trotted unusually quick to the edge of the House-Berg. His droopy eyes had widened, his ears were on end, his nose stretched out as far as it could, as though it were trying to escape and dive into the water.

"What is it, Grover?" asked Hank, marvelling at the change in the usually placid hound.

There was a faint noise ahead, almost like something rippling against the surface of the water. Then several things happened at once.

A ray of sunlight burst from behind a gleaming white mountain range and spread serenely over the lake and the House-Berg. A guttural noise in Grover's throat turned into a deep bark that echoed around the empty landscape. And an enormous silver fish, as long as Hank's arm, shattered the tranquil surface of the lake and dived back down into its depths. As soon as it had disappeared, another fish a little way off burst from the dark depths of the lake and followed its cohort. Then another, and another. The lake was soon teeming with swarms of fish, splashing, diving, jumping, flying, on every side of the House-Berg, some even leaping onto the House-Berg's icy platform and floundering wildly.

Hank laughed a deep hearty laugh. He jumped and cried as the rain of fish poured over him. Grover was barking excitedly, running around the House-Berg as though he were but a young puppy again. And Ingrid was chuckling to herself at the sight of her two companions, all while extending her long body as much as she could to soak up the heat from the Sun. As a fish flew too close to her immense jaws, there would be a quick snap, followed by a noisy gulp.

Hank meanwhile had run inside the house, stumbling out with a net and a large club. While Grover wrestled with a wriggling cod in his jaws, Hank threw the net over a bunch of them that had floundered near the front porch, before taking his club and swinging it madly on the imprisoned catch. It got so out of hand that he knocked a few of the porch's railings off, almost bludgeoned Grover in the back of the head, and accidentally batted a few flying trout through the windows of the house! He only stopped when he missed the net and walloped his own foot! His thick boots stopped him from breaking any bones, but it was still quite sore for the rest of the day.

***

The Sun shone brightly over the lake. The sky and the snow were so white that it was difficult to tell which was which. An iceberg bobbed gently on the calm, cool water. Atop it lay a ramshackle house of splintery wood with smashed windows and a dragon lying on the roof, dozing gently in the warm light. In front of the house, a man sat on a crooked chair, occasionally stoking a fire that cooked a carp on a spit. An old dog slept at the man's feet, occasionally letting out a light snore. The ice won't last forever. The dragon's wings will eventually heal. If the house doesn't sink first, it will gradually fall apart. But for now, they allowed themselves to rest and enjoy the day, enjoy being alive. The House-Berg simply rocked on the serene lake in the golden sunlight.

The Rain Dragon

By Dibyasree Nandy

Coveted the lune,
Her flowing, silver garb
Bedecked with stardust and dewy pearls
A crown of moonflowers.
The palace blindingly white
Pillars encircled by diamond vines,
From the porcelain balcony she gazes below
The tides obeying.

In a land where folk prayed to dragons,
The gods shifted form,
Winged, scaled creatures of stone; divine men and women
They blessed all, walking, mingling, their silhouettes new.

"Raise your head," the priests wept,
"You who govern over the waters azure,"
The serpentine deity unmoving, silent
"Cease the terror of the seas,
For ships fall prey,
What spells your wrath?
O Sapphire Dragon!"

Beneath the indigo ocean,
A pavilion stands
Birthed out of corals and shells of the shore
Fish swarming in and out
Emerald shrubs softly shimmering.
His poignant turquoise eyes,
Resplendent in garments blue, sewn out of marine thread of
lapis lazuli.
Turbulent, the soul of the ruler of the Deep
Moonlight glistens on the surface of the nightly foam
He yearns but he cannot fly,
Plumes too heavily soaked.

The clerics fell to their knees
Before the Dragon of the Moon,
"Why do you not show your face?
This eternal eclipse you have cursed us with!
Lovely princess of the sky?"

Her tears, lashes long,
Descend as a deluge
The waves roar, crashing
His longing and desire.
And thus, it is born, the offspring of the sterling downpour
and the fiery passion of the brine,
A dragon of rain,
A young shape-shifter, hydrangeas blooming at his feet,
Peacocks welcoming with feathers spread,
Lotuses drifting, swans turning to greet

The flood subsided; storms faded.
Rocks gathered, chisels brought,
Old pantheons washed away; a teal dragon reshaped.

The Wormwood Play
By Ben Sawyer

Albin was just a few short yards from the village when somebody shot at him. Not a good start to a day he was already dreading, he had to admit.

He reached down into the damp mire of melting snow and chilled mud and plucked up the arrow that had landed at his feet. He inspected the smooth shaft and broad head, let the fletching run along his fingers. It was a good hunting arrow, well made. But it had been fired to miss on purpose and had not been followed by others. There were always small mercies.

"This how you welcome visitors?" he asked, not looking in the direction the arrow had come from.

"Don't get many strangers round here," a young voice replied.

Albin smiled, and turned to face his persecutor. She stood by the side of the road, a second arrow nocked to her bow. Eyes screwed up in concentration glared at him under the crudely stitched wolf pelt of her hood.

"Who are that lot, then?" he asked, and cocked his head in the direction of the village. A line of wagons and beasts were crawling through the mud to get to the bustling settlement ahead. She rolled her eyes at getting caught out.

"Yeah, I just thought that sounded good," she said, and lowered her bow. "You're here for the Midwinter Festival, I suppose."

"In a manner of speaking," he said, and walked on.

***

The streets of the village of Wormwood heaved with people, jostling for position in the busy streets and yelling their barters to the occupants of merchants' wagons. Strange and enticing scents cut through the winter air, and money changed hands at pace.

A makeshift stage had been erected in the town square, and had drawn much of the crowd to it. Two men in crudely made wicker headdresses exchanged rhyming couplets that produced howls of delighted recognition from those watching their performance. There was little such joy for Albin – the show merely inspired thoughts of what had brought him here. But this one had been put off long enough, as he had told himself repeatedly for the best part of a month now. It did not make it a less daunting prospect.

The player with an imitation of a knight's helm was posturing, while his dragon-headed companion was roaring and flapping his green cloak. But it was the man in the crowd stood directly in front of Albin who was the focus of his attention right now. Thankfully, this individual's own gaze was consumed by the play at the expense of everything else.

Albin sidled a careful step closer, placing his feet in the quietest spot he could find, with no slurp of grubby snow or

164

crunch underfoot to announce his presence. He gave the crowd a quick scan, making sure their eyes were all on the stage, right where he wanted them to stay. Then slowly, carefully, he reached for the leather pouch tied oh-so-carelessly at the other man's waist.

"You enjoying the play?" came a voice at his elbow, and he pulled his arms in tight. He turned to see the girl who had shot at him stood at his side. How much she had seen he could only guess.

On stage, the dragon wrapped his arms around the knight, who vanished beneath the cloak. They shook from side to side with much melodramatic roaring before two shafts of wicker burst through the fabric. The knight then leapt free, clutching a bolt of red cloth. A third player, crawling on all fours and wearing a wicker dog's head, took the end of the cloth in his teeth and ran back and forth.

"I'm so confused," said Albin as the crowd roared their appreciation.

"Do you not know the story?" she asked, incredulous at such a gap in his education. "You're from the capital, aren't you? Thought you sounded city. You ever been to Wormwood before?"

"Once," he said, quietly indulging her. If she had seen his attempt at robbery, it did not seem to bother her. "Go on, tell me your local legend."

"Right, so the dragon is too tough for any kind of normal weapon to harm," she explained. "So Sir Roger, he puts big spikes all over his armour. Then the dragon grabs him and impales itself on the spikes, only when I was a kid, it were so much better than this 'cause there was blood everywhere…"

"And the dog?"

"Well, the dragon starts coming back to life, so he's got to chop it into bits. Then he gets his dog to carry the pieces as far away as possible. Oh, then the ending's dead sad…"

The dog and knight were reunited in the centre of the stage, their monster-slaying apparently done. The knight crouched down to his faithful friend, who made great play of licking his master's face. Both actors pulled ludicrous pained expressions and clutched at their throats, then collapsed on their backs, kicking their legs in the air until they finally lay still.

"Dragon guts are poisonous, obviously," she added. "So maybe not the best plan. Poor dog."

"And where's all this supposed to have happened?"

"Dragon Hill, just to the north of here."

"Dragon Hill?" he asked, a smile creasing his face. "Put a lot of thought into that one, did they?"

"We live in a place called Wormwood, names aren't what we do best!" she protested. "Anyway, if you had a hill that a dragon used to live on, what would you call it?"

"Fair point," he admitted. "But if you don't mind me saying, I wouldn't believe all of that story. Thanks for not shooting at me this time."

He walked away from her once again, confident that he knew all he needed. That wouldn't make tonight any easier. If he was right, it could only be so much the harder.

"Oi, thief!"

He tensed up, fearing that she had seen his pickpocketing after all. He turned and prepared to run, only to see her gesturing to the arrow he was still holding.

"That's mine, thank you!" she huffed. "I've gotta look after those!"

"Is that what your dad tells you?" he asked, as he held out the weapon point first. She whipped it from his hand, the feathers whistling, and stuffed it into the quiver at her hip.

"I don't give a stuff what that bugger says, whoever he is. I just know I've gotta eat. What you staring at?"

He hadn't realised he had been, but something had caught his attention about the girl, and he struggled to place what.

"Oh, nothing," he said, brushing off his concerns. "So what name did the people who can't name anything give to you?"

"Gemette Belfox," she declared as dramatically as the actors taking their bows behind her. "Huntress of the winter woods."

She strode off with head held high, utterly oblivious to the look of horror that had passed across his face when she gave her last name. He barely caught a breath until she was out of sight. This was a complication too far.

Once, he had said. And yet you can make a big difference to a place when you only visit it once.

***

An icy night had fallen on the village and driven the crowds away. Visitors able to return home had dispersed, those who remained had found what shelter they could before dark. Only one remained on the streets.

Albin stuffed hands deep into his coat pockets and fingered the meagre coins he had pilfered over the course of the day. Pieces of something larger, he thought as the metal rolled against his numb skin. It was a familiar story and not a promising one. If he was lucky, this really had just become a legend. But luck had never been one of his best attributes, a fact this village was determined to remind him of at every turn. Steeling himself, he walked north.

"Where you off to?"

Albin reflected that she was way too good at sneaking up on him. He turned to look at her ruefully, and pulled up the defences he had sworn to gather if she ever came back.

"Your mum know you're out here?" he asked, and Gemette snorted dismissively.

"Mum, dad, you're always on about that," she sneered. "You know, someone who thinks I'm just a kid could get an arrow somewhere very uncomfortable."

The word orphan floated through his mind, and conflicting emotions fought over which one got to keep it.

"Why do you keep following me?" he asked, positively dreading the answer.

"City, in't you?" she said with a shrug. "Don't get that round here. I've never been to a city."

"Go home," he said and walked off, hearing the less than stealthy footsteps of the huntress of the winter woods crunching through the snow behind him.

"Er, no," she protested. "Anyway, it's dangerous out there. You might run into bandits who'll rob a fancy city bloke blind.

And there'll be loads of them, and you'll be stuffed, but then… whoosh!"

She mimed firing the bow slung across her back. "Arrow out of the night, get the biggest one in the neck!" she declared proudly. "They don't know who's out there and they scarper! Gemette Belfox to the rescue!"

"If you come with me," he asked. "They'll get both of us, so how are you supposed to rescue me in the nick of time?"

"Oh," she said, crestfallen as her scenario collapsed beneath the weight of logic. "Can I just come anyway? I mean, where are you going?"

"If you must know, I'm going to the hill," he sighed, patience slowly being whittled away under her enthusiastic blows.

"Dragon Hill?!" she shouted, and he gestured frantically for her to lower her voice. They both took a moment to assess that nobody had been disturbed before continuing the conversation at a lower level. "From the play?"

"Yes," he hissed. "Why are you excited, you live here?"

"'Cause we're not supposed to go there!"

"Why not?"

"'Cause a bloody great dragon used to live up there, that's why! Why are you going?"

Secrecy was proving impossible in the face of features that became more familiar the more he looked at them. "Look, there's something hidden on the hill. That's why I'm here, to take it back to the Capital."

"Oh my stars, you work for the king, don't you?" she said excitedly. "What's up there?"

"Oh, pissing hellfire," he sighed, rubbing his face with both hands. "If I tell you, will you go away?"

"Yeah, right," she cackled derisively at the suggestion.

"I'm here for the sword of Sir Roger," he said with deathly seriousness. "And if you tell anyone, they'll just laugh at you. Now go home, wherever that is."

He resumed his journey, and heard the familiar footsteps behind him once more.

"Oh come on, I can't miss the sword of Sir Roger!" she protested. "And it'll probably be dangerous, so you'll need me to watch your back! And stick arrows in everyone else's!"

Albin sighed, realising there was no possibility of victory. That was something else that was proving all too familiar.

***

Dragon Hill stood alone beneath the stars, a single smooth dome rising from flat empty fields that spread out for miles around. Snow had settled in pale clumps on the writhing spiky brush that dotted its surface. Albin crouched down at the foot of the hill, and extended a hand to the rough shale pathway that stretched and wound up ahead of him. Satisfied, he began the ascent, before looking back to see Gemette shuffling from foot to foot behind him.

"Go back," he said, and meant it as a kindness this time.

"No, it's just," she grappled for an explanation. "Force of habit. Stay there, I'm coming."

They climbed up the steeply sloping hillside, feet crunching and slipping through the layers of loose stone and drifting snow. Albin followed the path, but as they drew closer to the top, Gemette broke off, scrambling up the steep slope alongside, hands and feet clawing for purchase. A desire to warn her of danger erupted unbidden into his mind, but by then she was standing tall and triumphant at the very top of the hill.

"Come on, old man!" she shouted, beckoning him onward. "You owe me a sword!"

He stifled a laugh as he came to the crest of the hill, then paused as he saw the three figures gathered around them. Gemette caught the look on his face, and spun on her heel, getting an arrow to her bow swiftly. A low growling filled the hillside, as the three figures stepped forward, their heads huge and imposing and framed with strange shapes. Horns, pointed ears and a billowing red plume that was cast in a trail across the sky. The dragon, the dog, and the knight. The players had come to perform.

"You shouldn't be here," the knight said in a deep, dark tone. His companions responded with harsh guttural barks. Their frosted breath exploded in thick white bursts. Albin sized them up and had a horrible feeling they weren't wearing their masks. Stolen pieces. He had feared as much.

"We don't want any trouble," Albin said, raising his hands as he walked slowly forward.

"Yeah, you'd better clear off, or I'll have you!" Gemette contributed, her aim switching back and forth between the three figures.

"Have you ever shot a man with that, child?" the knight asked.

"Bigger'n you and they'll not forget."

The knight laughed, his voice echoed by a gravelly hooting and hollering from his companions. Albin's eyes focused through the darkness but they remained shadows of what they had been and what they had taken from. It was an old story, but there were only three. Still more than he was prepared for.

"How old are you?" the knight asked.

"Eighteen," Gemette replied with a little too much pride.

"No you're not," Albin said without thinking.

"Sixteen!"

"Try again."

"How do you know how old I am?!" she sputtered angrily, the arrow shaking against her fingers. The others were circling now. Inhuman gibbers and growls pulsed from their great heads in bursts of fog that carried a whiff of red meat to Albin's nose. Unnaturally long fingers flexed at the end of their hands. Whatever they had taken, it had been with them a long time and left its mark.

"Look, she's just a kid, alright?" Albin argued calmly. "You've got nothing to gain from harming her, just let her go back to the village."

"Yeah, you'd better listen to him!" Gemette pitched in unhelpfully. "He's a king's man!"

"Is that what he told you?" the knight said, casually walking closer. "A king's man. A servant of the crown come to the wilds to do his majesty's will among the peasants. Is that what you are?"

"Well, I never said…" he protested, as Gemette's eyes widened with disappointment.

"He's a common thief, girl," the knight mocked, his concealed eyed somehow locking mercilessly onto hers. "While he watched our play, we watched his. Waiting his moment to steal from some witless merchant. And then you interrupted his sport. But that didn't stop him taking what he could from your neighbours."

"Is that true?" Gemette whispered, swallowing hard on a world both bigger and smaller than her expectations.

"He's a cutpurse, bound for a gibbet," the knight said. "Who is here seeking treasure."

"Yeah, to take it back to the king, right?" Gemette asked, glaring directly at Albin. For the second time in his life, he watched trust vanish from those eyes.

"I said the capital," Albin said after a moment. "I never said the king."

"The king is the biggest cutpurse of them all," the knight added, and gently reached out to pluck the arrow from Gemette's bow. "But he knows nothing of this one. Begone, child. This is not for you."

The girl's jaw clenched hard on her anger, as she glanced from Albin to the knight to the two monstrous figures in the shadows, before stomping away down the path. Albin did not dare to turn and watch her go. The dragon player was behind him now, he could feel it. Smoky breath and low growling called to his senses.

"You know why I'm here," he said. "You know what has to be done."

"The beast rests forever," the knight replied. "Its strength has passed to men."

"To you."

"To men," he repeated, and a grunt broke from the lips of the hound. The dragon player placed a heavy ridged hand on Albin's shoulder, and iron-hard nails dug into his flesh.

"Yes, but the men who seem to be wielding this strength right now happen to be you three, so my point stands," Albin protested through a gasp of pain as the claws drew blood. "I don't see you sharing it around. Pieces chopped from the dragon, and scattered, that's how the story goes. But they weren't just scattered, were they?"

"They are us," the knight said. "They are always us. The children of the dragon."

"Yes, but now it's time! You must feel it."

"We know," said the knight. "And we know it shall not have what it needs while we stand."

"Oh, I was afraid you'd say that."

The knight nodded, and the dragon player spun Albin around to look into a face once human, now framed with bony irregular horns. The pieces of the dragon torn away by Sir Roger had done their work on those who took them.

His skin was warped into a pattern of mottled scales around eyes that glowed from firelight within, split by a vertical line of black. Pale membranes slid back and forth across the glossy surface.

Dragon guts are poisonous, Albin reflected. But in more ways than one.

Thin lips peeled back over rows of needle teeth, and the dragon player lashed out hard, the blow sending Albin staggering to the ground. Before he could right himself, the player had seized him by the throat and lifted him off his feet. He struggled to pull a thin trickle of icy air into his lungs as the beast that was nothing human distended its jaw wide, and hissed its fury into the night. Which was right when the arrow erupted from its throat.

The glowing eyes widened as the light left them, and Albin was dropped to land clumsily. He looked up to see Gemette stood on the edge of the hillside, fumbling a second arrow into position. He could see her mind racing around how the actions she had predicted she would take tonight had come to pass, and what that truly meant.

As the player fell, a hissing erupted from the ground. Pale steam rose from his corpse and the distorted flesh flaked away, pieces sinking into the cold earth. Albin felt the hill shudder ever so slightly beneath him. His fingers brushed snow that was dissolving to water under the tremors that steadily grew in pace.

The ground cracked as he rolled over, and two huge clumps of earth burst upwards in a shower of displaced soil and fuming vapour. A tight triangular opening had emerged between the two chunks of the hill, and even from where he lay, Albin could feel the heat surging from within. He scrambled upright, diving in a low loping run towards the opening. Out of the corner of his eye, he saw the hound leaping, distended jaws wide, then heard the whistle of an arrow be answered by a squealing cry as the dog-faced man fell to the ground in a plume of steam.

Albin plunged into the opening. The sharp rock around him was warm to the touch and pulsed with something alive barely contained within it. In the centre of the chamber, a sword rose from where it had been driven hard into the ground, the steel pitted with age. He stretched aching fingers forward to grab at the hilt, when a blow landed hard into the back of his neck. He felt the great weight of the knight on him, his calm measured tones bursting into a frantic squealing that he spat through the face of his wicker helm.

"Mine!" he shouted, childhood claiming his whole demeanour. "Mine! Mine!"

Albin struggled to turn under the weight of his attacker, and saw Gemette following them into the cave. She scrambled forward, an arrow in her grip and stabbed hard into the knight's shoulder. Her blow was awkward and the arrow split under the weight of the impact. The knight turned, clutching at her with shuddering fingers.

Albin turned his attention back to the sword, gripping it tightly and pulling with the little strength he had. The blade ground against the surrounding rock, finally pulling free, followed by a trickle of viscous black fluid.

He swung the sword round and drove it hard into the knight's back. He fell to his knees with a gasp, frantically batting at his steaming chest, as Albin pushed past, grabbing Gemette by the hand and hauling her out of the opening while the ground tore and splintered around them. They half-ran and half-fell down the slope they had ascended, finally collapsing in a heap in the frozen mud surrounding the hill.

The ground trembled for miles around, as the hill seemed to grow, its dark mass rising higher and higher from the surrounding flatlands with waves of soil, rock and melting snow thundering down its smooth sloping sides. Albin pushed himself upright to watch, as the hillside nearest them rippled and flexed and finally exploded outwards.

It was as if a vast hand had erupted from the earth, with thin bony fingers extended for hundreds of feet across the night sky, terminating in sharp points. A membrane of translucent skin stretched across the spaces between, and even in the night, a hint of brilliant orange and pink colouring could be seen across it, a sheet of living flame under a cold moon.

A second of these shapes unfurled on the far side, the hooked thumbs clawing at the ground, which continued to lurch. The earth shook as the hill launched itself into the air. Gemette and Albin were tossed aside by the uproar, crashing to the ground followed by a rain of displaced earth and snow.

They looked up to see the dragon rise.

The hill unfurled itself, a long serpentine body stretching between the wings that had opened to carry it aloft. Four muscular legs coated in gleaming scales pawed the night air as a long neck stretched out, the great bony head unleashing a throaty roar that shook Albin to his bones.

It twisted and danced in the sky like a swift swooping for insects, but Albin could only look at Gemette. She stood directly underneath the dragon, her wide eyes cast upwards. She laughed and gasped and cried out in what felt like one continuous breath. There was no fear, only wonder at the legend made flesh.

After a few short moments, the great beast turned in the air and flew off, titanic wingbeats thudding against the darkness, disappearing to wherever it was bound. Albin allowed himself to rest at last, collapsing onto the hard, cracked earth. He placed a hand to his chest, and snarled at the slashes left by the transformed player's talons. His blood felt warm against the cold of everything else.

"You owe me a sword," he heard a voice say, and was snapped out of his reverie to see Gemette standing above him.

"You got a dragon out of it," he responded, clinging to flippancy in the face of the spectacular.

"It's just…" she said, trying to marshal the army of experiences brawling within her mind. "I thought you were a king's man, and then it turns out you're a cutpurse, and then you make a dragon happen! What are you?"

"I'm not a king's man," Albin sighed. "It might surprise you to learn that the king wouldn't be best pleased to have dragons flying around the place."

"Are you a cutpurse?"

Albin swallowed, and decided one truth would require silence from another, for now. So he gave the one that was asked for.

"When I have to be."

Gemette contemplated the truth presented to her, as her own wriggled in her belly.

"Did I kill a man tonight?" she said, her voice a small child's.

"No," he said, in all honesty. "There were no men with us tonight. That was something else. Something that should never have been."

Gemette turned to the direction the dragon had flown, squinting to make out its shape against the dark sky.

"Where will it go?" she asked.

"Wherever it wants," Albin said. "And long past time. You want to know what I am, well, I make things like this happen. I raise the beasts up out of the legends and let them be free again. I can barely believe it myself sometimes, but there you go."

Gemette turned back to him, with her mother's eyes.

"Why?"

"Because it needs to happen," he said. "Because otherwise we all end up like them."

"Will you do it again?" she asked, pondering the next step.

"Yes."

She smiled and he could see the next question forming on her face, and decided, despite himself, that the answer to that would be yes as well. And maybe when she figured out the other question, he'd be ready to answer.

The Dragon of the Bailey

By J D Byrne

Lhai sniffed the water in his trough. Was the poison in there? He couldn't tell. He cursed, not for the first time, that the Maker had given dragons such a poor sense of smell. What if he just didn't drink it? How could they make him? He was as large as any of the guards. Bigger, if one counted his tail. His rough grey hide would be difficult for spears or swords to pierce. What could they do if he would not drink? But, then again, how could he refuse when he was so very thirsty?

He extended his wings, stretching nearly nine feet now from end to end. The cobalt blue feathers had come in fuller and thicker this time. It had been easy for him to swoop up to the perch yesterday afternoon, probably too easy. If he had resisted the urge to be away from these humans for a while, to sit above them and keep watch over their activities, maybe his keeper would have forgotten about the clipping. Another few days and perhaps he could have flown over the wall and away from this bailey. But his regular water and food disappeared a few days ago and the keeper would not let Lhai out of his sight. The clipping was near. His keeper was not so forgetful.

But now it was too late, and he was so very thirsty. He drove his head into the trough and gulped furiously, knowing that a deep sleep would soon overtake him.

When he woke up, Lhai could feel the cold iron and leather muzzle that had been wrapped around his face for the ceremony. It took a few moments before he remembered where he was and for the throbbing pain in his wings to come to the fore. He gritted his teeth and tried to stand, but was stopped by a sharp yank on the chain that lashed him to the stone pedestal.

To one side, keeping a safe distance, was a priest. He held a large, worn, brown book in his hands and smiled nervously at Lhai when their eyes met.

To the other side, at the same distance but looking much more certain of himself, sat the one they called Lord Kala. He looked bored by the state of affairs, as if he had something better to do. Lhai hoped his unconsciousness had delayed the proceedings, just to be difficult.

Out in front of him, Lhai could see the crowd that had gathered in the courtyard below, huddled together against the damp morning mist that was so prevalent in these parts. There were a few dozen people, ringed by another dozen guards in polished armor, creating a makeshift fence out of tall, golden spears. What the Maker had taken from the nose, She had given to the ear, but the crowd murmured to itself, making it difficult for Lhai to hear the contents of any one conversation.

The crowd hushed when the priest raised the book high over his head and began to intone the prayer. Lhai had heard it six times before, every year on the anniversary of his capture, a day that also happened to be Kala's birthday. For Kala, the coincidence made Lhai's captivity all the more auspicious. For Lhai, it was a cruel joke. The public never saw his wings getting clipped, never saw the real reason he could not leave the castle.

"And so the Maker, who is just and gracious," the priest said, slowly and deliberately, "did promise that should any dragon come to your castle, then should you know peace and happiness."

"Get on with it," Kala said, slumped in his chair.
The priest picked up the pace, as ordered. "And so long as the dragon remains in your castle, the lord of that castle shall rule, with justice and mercy to his people." The lines were well worn and got little reaction from the scrum.

As the priest continued, Lhai's eyes caught some movement near the back of the crowd. He focused on a young boy, no more than nine years old, tugging urgently on the arm of the old man who stood beside him.

"Grandfather," the boy said, in a loud whisper that was drowned out by the priest's speech for everyone save Lhai. The old man tried to shush him, but the boy kept on. "Why does it wear a muzzle? Why is it chained down? If it wants to stay, why does it . . ." The old man put an end to the questions with a swift smack up the side of his head.

Lhai grinned, as best he could.

***

One benefit to having his wings clipped was that, for a few weeks afterward, Lhai was free to roam the bailey without much oversight. Each day he would struggle up to his perch on the inner wall and survey the activities of the humans.

He kept an eye out in particular for the boy who had so many questions. Lhai watched one day as the boy ran with great purpose to and fro around the bailey, slipping in between people twice his size. He was not playing; he was working, apparently as a runner for someone. He knew this place well, better than a boy of his age should.

One day, when the boy stopped by the well for a drink, Lhai flapped awkwardly down from his perch and landed on the stone wall of the well, a few feet away. The boy did his best to avoid looking his direction.

"You work hard, boy," Lhai said, trying his best to smooth out the natural rasp in his voice.

The boy turned to him, his eyes wide and mouth agape. He quickly looked away and took another drink.

"Now, now," Lhai said, shuffling along the wall toward the boy, "there is no need to worry. I am not going to hurt you."

The boy stopped drinking, like he was mulling over the proposition, but did not look at the dragon.

"I know you have questions. How can I answer them if you will not talk to me, boy?"

"Lessard," the boy said, after a deliberative pause. "My name is Lessard."

"Ah, he speaks! You may call me Lhai, Lessard. So, what do you want to know?"

Lessard looked around to see if anyone was watching them. "Grandfather says you are dangerous, to stay away."

Lhai sat back on his haunches, doing his best to look more like an oversized mongrel dog than a dragon. "Do I look dangerous to you?"

They continued like this, talking a bit every day when the boy stopped to get a drink. One day, Lessard leaned in particularly close. "Can you breathe fire?"

Lhai grinned. "What do you think?"

"My grandfather told me so," Lessard said. "A single dragon could burn an entire village down."

"If I could breathe fire, why would I still be here?" Lhai asked. "Your grandfather has, no doubt, heard many things in his long life and is most wise, but not everything he has heard is the truth."

Lessard looked indignant. "Are you calling him a liar?"

"No, no, young friend," Lhai said, in his best soothing voice. "One need not be a liar to be wrong about something, only misinformed. That is no sin." He thought otherwise, actually, but he could not antagonize the boy.

Over the days, Lessard asked more questions borne of his grandfather's tales.

"Do you live forever?" he asked one dreary afternoon.

"No, of course not," Lhai said. "Everything must come to an end. That is the way the Maker made the world. But we do live a very long time, compared to humans."

"How do you remember it all?" Lessard asked. "Your whole long life?"

184

"The Maker has blessed us with great memories," Lhai said. "Once we have seen something, or heard someone say something, we will never forget it. One day, long in the future, when you are as old as your grandfather, I will remember our talks perfectly."

Another day, Lessard asked if Lhai had a store of treasure buried somewhere deep in a mountain.

Lhai chuckled. "Not all dragons live in mines or caves," he said. "But we do like to live apart from each other and apart from humans. And, yes, your grandfather is right about the treasure. Live a long life and you, too, will accumulate many things." He did not mention that his own cache was surely gone now, with no one to protect it all these years.

One day, it was Lhai who asked the questions. "You always talk of your grandfather," he asked, "but what of your mother or father?"

Lessard took a slow drink. "My father was killed. In one of Lord Kala's battles. It was a long time ago, just after I was born."

Lhai did his best to look sympathetic. "And your mother?"

Lessard stared into the well for a long time. "She's gone."

"Gone?"

"Just gone," Lessard said, walking away.

Finally, one day when the clinging rain of the morning finally came to an end, Lessard asked the question Lhai had been waiting and hoping for. "If you have wings, why don't you fly away?"

Lhai hopped down off of the well and spread his wings wide, partly blocking the sunlight. "Look closely at these wings, Lessard. What do you see?"

The boy scanned the bailey, cautiously, to see if anyone else was looking, then stepped closer and peered at Lhai's left wing. "Feathers," he said. "Like a bird. So you should be able to fly."

Lhai nodded. "Look closer. Does something look wrong about them?" He waved the left wing around a bit.

Lessard backed away. "They're so short. Why?"

"Because," he said, wrapping his wings down along his back, "they are clipped every few weeks, to keep them that way."

"Who does that?" Lessard asked, a puzzled look on his face.

"My keeper," Lhai said. "I do not know his name. But I do know he does it on the orders of Lord Kala."

Lessard stood there, mouth partly open but saying nothing, for a few seconds. "Why would Lord Kala do that?"

Lhai moved a bit closer and whispered, "Because if my feathers grew back completely, I would be able to fly away from here."

"But," Lessard started to say, then stopped himself. "But, you stay here because it is the Maker's blessing upon Lord Kala's reign."

Lhai slowly shook his head. "If it is truly the Maker's will that I remain here, why must Lord Kala do this?" He unfurled his wings again. "I am a prisoner, Lessard, just as much as the petty thieves in the dungeon. It makes no difference that I am not chained every day. What is Lord Kala afraid of?"

Lessard said nothing more, only took another long drink, then ran off. Lhai flapped awkwardly back up to his perch on the wall and smiled, just slightly. He didn't want anyone else to think he might be pleased.

***

That night the full moon was obscured, passing clouds casting a shifting white glow over the castle. Lhai had settled into an empty cart, enjoying its soft straw, when he saw a figure walking across the bailey. It was Lessard, doing his best to move without arousing suspicion.

"Psst, boy!" Lhai said in a loud whisper. "Lessard!"

The boy changed course and jogged silently to the wagon.

"What are you doing up at this time of night?" Lhai asked.

In the pale moonlight, Lessard's young face looked tense and haggard. "I can't sleep. Can't keep from thinking about," he said, nodding toward Lhai's folded wings.

"That is kind of you," the dragon said, "but it is not your concern, you know."

"It is," Lessard said, passionately. "The priests and grandfather say that what Lord Kala does, he does on all our behalf."

Lhai decided to play along. "Still, you are just a young boy. I appreciate your sympathy, but . . ."

Lessard shook his head to cut him off. "This is wrong," he declared firmly. "They shouldn't do that to anybody, what they do to you."

Lhai tried hard not to grin widely at the boy. He had come around more quickly that he could have hoped.   "But what can you do against the strength of Lord Kala and his men?"

The boy thought for a moment. "How long would it take for your feathers to grow back? All the way back, I mean?"

"Not long, perhaps another week," Lhai said, "but they will get clipped again in a few days."

"And once your feathers have grown back, you can fly away?"

Lhai nodded. "Yes, I think so. It has been so long since I have truly flown, but I think I could."

"Then all we need is a place to hide you," Lessard said. "Let me think about it." He turned and left without another word.

Two nights later, Lessard again came to Lhai while he rested in the cart. "I've found a place," he said, waving for the dragon to follow him.

Lhai dutifully obliged, trailing Lessard to a spot where one of the bailey's inner walls met the high outer rock wall of the castle. The boy fell to his knees and clawed earth out from the foot of the wall with his hands. In a few moments he had dug a hole, big enough to wiggle loose a stone in the inner wall.

"There," he said, pointing to the hole in the wall.

Lhai crouched down and peered inside, slipping his long neck into the hole. "What is that?"

"It's a back room, locked behind a door, in the blacksmith's shop. It's storage. I don't think he's been inside in years." Lessard looked at the dragon. "It's a place for you to hide."

Lhai examined the hole again. It was small, but he could fit through it, with some effort. "All right," he said. "Then what?"

"You stay there as long as it takes for your feathers to grow back," Lessard said. "Then I'll let you out and you can fly away."

It seemed very simple when the boy said it. "Will they not come and look there?" Lhai gestured toward the hole and the small room beyond it.

Lessard grinned. "Trust me. I've spent a lot of time in that room. If you don't want to be found, that's the place."

Lhai looked around and considered his options. "I suppose there is no reason to wait then, eh?" He began to shimmy his way through the hole. It was a tighter fit that he imagined, the rough edges of the stone scraping against his hide as he went through. It wasn't pleasant, but he could do it again, when the time came.

"How long should I wait?" Lessard asked, already piling the dirt back into position, as if closing the last spot of Lhai's tomb.

"A week," Lhai said, "but no more. I will be starving by then."

"A week," Lessard agreed, then slowly moved the stone back into the hole.

***

The room was cold, dark, and damp, but it suited Lhai's purpose. It was such an unpleasant place, he couldn't imagine anyone making more than a cursory examination of it. He felt bad for Lessard, who must have been very eager for solitude to subject himself to it.

189

The walls were made of stacked stones, between which there were numerous cracks and crevices. It was not enough to light the room, but enough sunlight filtered through for Lhai to mark the passing of the days. It also allowed enough sound to seep through that Lhai could follow the goings on outside.

The hue and cry had gone up in the morning after Lessard hid him, not long after the sun rose. There was shouting and the sound of pounding feet running all around the bailey. The next day there must have been an assembly of some kind, as Lhai heard Lord Kala address his subjects. He called for calm in this moment of uncertainty. When someone asked what it meant that the dragon was missing, Kala said only that "it means dragons are very willful creatures. That is why its choosing to live here brings with it the Maker's blessing."

Fearing that his sanctuary might be discovered, Lhai went to a long, low bench that ran along the far wall. He was able to reposition the items stored underneath it and slide into the empty space. With his teeth he pulled a ragged blanket up over him. He made himself as small, as still, and as quiet as possible. Then he waited.

In his hiding place, deep within an already well hidden room, Lhai began to lose track of time. He didn't know whether it was later that same day or the next when the guards came. First he heard a mass of voices. There was so much commotion in the bailey, he didn't pick them out specifically at first, but he heard them growing closer and clearer.

Finally, he heard a baritone voice, the captain of Kala's guard, berating someone on the other side of the door, charging him with the most grave of offenses. Lhai took a deep breath and tried as best he could to squeeze into an even smaller space.

The door thundered open, thudding hard against one of the many bits of furniture and debris piled around the room.

"In there!" shouted the captain, "what's in there?"

"Just junk," said the blacksmith, voice fluttering nervously. Lhai almost felt bad for him.

Feet moved in and around the room, heavy steps clomping on the dirt floor. There were several guards, at least three, plus the one who had been yelling. Lhai heard one of the guards step not six inches away from him. Instinctively, he flinched, enough that the blanket fell away, partly exposing his head.

One pair of feet turned and walked toward the bench, beside which another pair stood, motionless. Lhai swallowed hard, his heart pounding in his ears, then heard a loud thump from above him.

"What's that?" he heard the captain say. The blacksmith said nothing. "Don't you know that Lord Kala has prohibited any idols of the old gods? You're not a blasphemer, are you?"

"No, no, of course not," said the blacksmith. "It's just a token. A family heirloom, really. It's just a small thing, it fits in the palm of your hand. Nobody ever has to know it's here. My father's father, you see . . ." He was cut off by what sounded like a smack across the face.

"Yes, well, we'll have to take it with us," the guard said. "Anything else?"

The two standing in front of Lhai murmured to each other, and then to the captain, that there was nothing else here.

"Right, then, let's get out of here," the captain said.

Lhai watched as the feet only a few inches from him turned and marched back toward the door. In short order it slammed closed again and Lhai felt the fear and tension melt away from him. He didn't know how much more of this he could take.

***

Lhai stayed stock still in his hiding place, curled up so tightly that he shook. His throat was dry and his stomach ached. Every noise made him clench and catch his breath. He lost track of the days. How much longer before Lessard would come to let him out? When he heard the guards return and rough up the blacksmith just outside the door, he knew he could wait no longer.

Once they were gone, Lhai emerged from his refuge and carefully felt his way around the wall, searching for the loose block. When he found the one that just ever so slightly jutted out from the wall, he took a tenuous hold of it with his talons and began to pull. The rock was dry and slick and wedged tightly in the wall: his talons slipped off, sending him tumbling backwards. He redoubled his efforts, working more carefully to pry the block slowly out of its spot.

When the block was moved, he began to dig, throwing great heaps of dirt behind him. He could hear the sound of voices around, but did not give them much attention. Light began to creep through the hole the more earth he moved. It was

192

daytime, not the best time for an escape. Never mind – he could take no more of this.

When the hole was big enough, Lhai dove in, head first. It was a tight fit, but he managed to make it through, bursting out of the other side to see a gathering of people staring at him.

"The dragon!" murmured the crowd, wide smiles beginning to blossom on the faces.

Lhai knew he had only a few moments before Kala's men would come to put him in chains. It was time to do two things he had not done in all the years he had been held captive.

First, he took in a deep breath and unleashed a high, ragged, piercing shriek. It drove some of the assembled throng running, while others covered their ears. The smiles instantly disappeared. The mass of humanity stepped back, giving Lhai more room. It would surely bring the out the guards, but they would be coming anyway. Either he escaped now or not at all.

Second, he raised his wings and extended them fully, sweeping the air in front of him and driving the crowd back a bit more. He took a quick glimpse left and right and smiled. With great up and down strokes Lhai beat his wings and slowly began to lift off the ground, quickly gaining momentum. He shrieked again, just for good measure.

Lhai rose into the air, more easily than he had in years. His wings ached, sending shots of pain down his back. He gritted his teeth and beat them again, trying to push through the hot aching of muscles that had lain dormant for so long. Drawn by the commotion, a squad of Kala's guards ran across the bailey and stared, mouths open, as Lhai rose slowly, five feet then ten feet into the air.

Lhai caught a glimpse of something shiny, the sun glinting off metal, out of the corner of his eye. He turned and saw one of the guards notching an arrow in his bow. Lhai beat his wings harder and began to make for the wall. He needed another fifteen feet to clear it, but he could feel his weight dragging behind him.

"You idiot!" the captain shouted.

Lhai looked over his shoulder and saw the captain smacking the bow out of the guard's hand. "We've just found it and now you want to kill it?"

Lhai smirked, knowing that a single arrow could not kill him, but if it somehow happened to pierce his hide it would slow him down, which he couldn't afford right now. He took a deep breath and drove, with all his strength, toward the top of the outer wall. He rose higher and higher — first to the level of his perch, then to the top of the rampart - as he closed in on the wall. But he realized, nearly too late, that he did not yet have the height to carry him over.

Before he hit the wall, Lhai executed a long-banked turn, so that he faced the bailey and the assembled crowd below. He stopped beating his wings and began to fall, just for a split second. Then he extended them again and swooped down over the bailey, plunging toward the crowd. The dive both caused them to scatter and gave Lhai needed speed. It also allowed him to see Lessard, hiding from the rushing crowd near the well. Lhai tried to give him a nod, some kind of acknowledgement, but he also saw some of the guard hustling back to the bailey with ropes and nets.

Lhai knew this was his last chance. He dove down to about five feet, gaining speed as he went, then banked hard back up toward the outer wall. He beat his wings with swift, powerful strokes, gaining height as he charged to the wall. The smooth, dry fibers of a rope smacked against a back foot, but failed to hold. This was too close.   He had come out too early.

The wall loomed ahead of him, the top just out of reach. Lhai knew he couldn't risk another dive down into the bailey. This was his last chance. He held his breath and gave his wings one last desperate push. He did not fly, unfettered, over the edge as he had so often dreamt. Instead, he came up just short, but managed to reach out and grab the top of the wall with his front talons. Gasping for breath, every muscle in his body burning, he pulled up and threw himself over, to the outside.

He had climbed up and over the wall furthest from the main gate, which only now was being opened to allow his pursuers out. Lhai took a deep breath and glided toward the nearest clump of woodland, trying to recover his strength. He knew there was no catching him now. He picked up his aching wings again and began to beat them in a slow consistent rhythm, powering out over the treetops. He was free.

***

Lhai circled high overhead, riding the gusts of warm air rising from the fires below. He wove his way around tall columns of black smoke, trying to see what he could.

Lord Ziaud had been all too happy to receive him, given that he was willing to listen to any inside information about his rival, Kala. But Lhai was quick to assure Ziaud this was not a business dealing. He was no spy. This was personal. Ziaud agreed to give Lhai safe passage in out and out of his castle, for the price of information. Over a long meal of finely roasted goat, Lhai had told him all he knew and heard about Lord Kala's defenses. He told him about the number of fighters in the company, how poorly led they were and how easily frightened. And he told Ziaud about the walls and of the weak spot near his hiding place.

Ziaud was easily convinced of Lhai's story of confinement. "Kala always did hold symbolism over strength. Like those gold painted spears," he said. "Just like him to find a dragon and put it in shackles."

Armed with Lhai's information, Ziaud needed little prodding to attack Kala. He had wanted to do so for years, but hadn't known enough of the details of Kala's company to be certain of victory. Ziaud was a conservative man, but one who would strike when the opportunity arose.

Lhai had given only one condition to Ziaud before he told all he knew. "There is a boy," he said, "named Lessard. He is the one who helped me."

"You want to ensure he is not hurt?" Ziaud asked.

"More than that," Lhai said. "He has no real family. After you finish with Kala, I doubt he will have anything left at all, especially if his grandfather does not survive the assault. Take him in. Give him a home. He will do right by you, I think."

Ziaud weighed the condition for a few moments.

"And under no circumstances are you to keep him prisoner," Lhai added.

"Very well," Ziaud said. "It is a small price to pay to be rid of Kala."

***

When the clang of steel on steel and the war cries of men in battle stopped, Lhai dropped slowly down toward Kala's castle. He alighted on the north wall, the one opposite the site of Ziaud's attack. The sounds of battle had given way to the sounds of grief and pain, of wounded men calling to the Maker for salvation, and of women weeping for those already gone. Ziaud's men gathered prisoners, marching small groups back and forth across the bailey.

Lhai could see that Kala was among them, bloodied from a gash above his eye. His prophecy had come true. The dragon had left the bailey and Kala's rule had come crashing down.

Away from the prisoners, amongst a group of soldiers standing under Ziaud's banner, stood Lessard. He looked small and helpless compared to the armored men around him, but Lhai knew better. He hung overhead until their eyes met, then smiled and flew away.

To Hear the Bats on Christmas Day

By Mary Jo Rabe

Maquoketa B. Dragon spread his muscular, green, athletic wings and tapped away at the keyboard in his office crevice in the lowest cavern of the Maquoketa Caves State Park. Still a young adult dragon, Maq kept his agile claws neatly trimmed, filing them daily on the firm, gray stalagmites covering the floor of the dark cave.

He needed his nimble fingers to operate all his communications devices. A modern dragon, living somewhat alone by choice, had to navigate his way among other sentient creatures, adapting to every technological advance, choosing which local customs to engage in and which to ignore.

Like all dragons, Maq had equal access to the material and the magical world, but he felt most at home here in the material Maquoketa Caves among the living creatures who were his neighbours.

Yes, there were several orders on his display for the beverages he produced in his brewing cave, all from steady and reliable customers who had paid in advance. No doubt, the humans were stocking up for their seasonal parties. Maq confirmed the orders and suggested times for pick-up after his nap. His scaly eyelids were starting to feel a little heavy.

Maq generally kept his office and residence somewhat dark except for the technical illumination that imitated blazing fires in the center of the vast cave as well as streams of water running down the walls.

The wind-powered air circulation in his caves was state-of-the-art. Other dragons clung to old-fashioned fires and genuine water in their caves. However, Maquoketa B. Dragon saw no advantage to enduring sooty or moldy walls in the place where he spent so much time. Dragons lived a long, long time; there was no need to risk damage to any dragonian body parts.

Maq liked to take care of business for an hour or so after returning from his nightly airborne constitutional. It was good exercise to fly and search for suitable morsels to munch on before he slept. Today he brought back an astonishingly plump doe he had snatched from the swamps surrounding the village of Green Island. It would do nicely for a timely bedtime snack.

As soon as the bats returned, he would nap for a few hours. The bats maintained more or less the same nocturnal lifestyle as he did, although they seemed to need more sleep.

The Maquoketa Caves were officially closed from October 15th to April 15th to protect the bats in their hibernation season.

Theoretically, December was a hibernation month for the bats, but Maq encouraged his bats to stay active all year round and let Maq forage for their food when they couldn't find enough fruit or insects. Yesterday he brought back a considerable volume of cherries, now fermenting nicely in their barrels. Eventually he would take them down to the brewing cave.

Maq was famous for the corn liquor he distilled from the homegrown Iowa ingredients, but he kept experimenting with other products he sold online. A financially successful dragon had to remain flexible.

The brown bats who resided in the caves were Maq's loyal friends as well as cavemates. They were amiable creatures, and Maq got along well with them.

He and the bats enjoyed many pleasant get-togethers at twilight and dawn in his home caves. They were a source of comfort when other creatures, including dragons, got on Maq's nerves.

Maq prided himself on staying informed by using modern technology. However, by swooping, swarming, and listening, the bats managed to pick up even more useful information concerning the Maquoketa Caves and surrounding regions.

They had their own names in bat language, but Maq B. allowed himself the indulgence of giving many of them nicknames in the local lingo. Apparently, a dragon's snout, though capable of speaking all the human languages without an accent, couldn't manage the contortions necessary for bat speak. Maq's attempts at speaking bat language with the bats only resulted in fits of high-pitched, hysterical, bat echolocation shrieks of laughter.

When the bats suddenly flew down into his cave this morning, they weren't laughing; they were shivering and shaking off snowflakes.

"It's a blizzard out there," Bat-Out-Of-Hell said.

"That must have come up suddenly," Maq said. "When I got back, there were clouds, and the air was bracingly chilly, but I didn't encounter any precipitation."

"I'm cold, soaked, and starving," Batshit-Crazy said. "We didn't find a thing to eat."

Maq flicked his gigantic tail and lifted the lids off ten barrels of cherries. "All yours, gang," he said. "Excellent quality fruit that you can garnish with the Mediterranean fruit flies you can see flying around the ceiling. Swallow as much as you can; it'll help you sleep."

The bats flew to the barrels and started slurping the fermenting cherries, interrupting their voracious imbibitions only to swoop up to the top of the cave and fill their mouths with fruit flies.

"Don't over-indulge," Batter-Up said. "We have to be sober enough to grasp the roosts hanging from the ceiling when we sleep."

"Killjoy," Bat-in-the-Belfry complained. "Our feet know what to do."

That turned out to be correct. The bats were soon fairly inebriated but had no trouble perching on the roosts and falling asleep once Maq helped them up there.

"The snow wasn't why we came back so soon," Bat Masterson slurred his words as he took off for a roost.

"Then what?" Maq asked. "Were there predators or idiots with guns outside?"

"No," Bat Masterson said. "It was the Christmas parties, the music, and the bells. Human beings invite all kinds of animals to join them celebrating their holiday, but not bats. When we tried to join in, they cursed us and tried to shoo us away. So we came home." He flapped his wings feebly, and Maq used his gigantic tail to lift the bat up to the roost.

That made Maq angry. He didn't have much use for human celebrations himself. He only invited other dragons to his parties. All of Maq's relatives were of the opinion that it was best to reveal the existence of dragons to as few human beings as possible. Most humans were simply too unpredictable and illogical to deal with.

This was different. The human beings had hurt the bats' feelings. Maquoketa B. Dragon didn't intend to let that pass. However, it did seem prudent to give the matter some thought rather than to just fly off and scorch a few small towns in the neighborhood in order to avenge the bats.

Hot-headed dragons often got into unnecessary trouble. It was better to first analyze any existing problem, calculate the consequences of possible actions, choose the best solution, and then act.

The problem, assuming Bat Masterson had articulated himself accurately, was that the bats wanted to be included in human Christmas celebrations but the human beings didn't want the bats around. Maq was now much too sleepy to do any serious thinking. He decided to take a long nap.

After a thoroughly recuperative snooze of several hours, Maq still didn't have any idea how to help the bats. He snorted a few tiny flames, hoping that that would help. Fortunately, his communication wall lit up before he could set anything in the cave on fire.

A male, human face somewhat hidden by a bushy, unkempt, grayish beard and mustache, was projected on an illuminated, side wall. "Hey, Maq," he said. "How are things going? Can I pick up my order of corn liquor tomorrow?"

That was Curtis, a regular, reliable customer who had never had qualms or misgivings about doing business with a dragon, part of his "live-and-let-live" philosophy about being a good neighbor. Over the decades, Curtis always made sure that the local farmers gave Maq top quality corn for his liquor.

"Of course," Maq said. "I think you'll find the liquor to be of especially high quality."

"As always," Curtis said. "Maq, would you ever consider increasing production of your corn liquor? I could sell ten times as much."

"I'll give it some thought," Maq said. "However, I prefer variety in my enterprises. Dragons need to avoid boredom."

"Just a thought," Curtis said. "Do whatever you need to do to keep producing whatever you can. And, if I can be of any help …"

"Actually," Maq admitted. "I have a problem and could use your input. The bats who live in these caves stopped hibernating some years ago because I was able to supply them with sufficient food during the winter months. It was probably selfish of me to encourage them to stay awake, but I enjoy their company. They are excellent companions for a dragon, observant but not too loquacious."

"That explains it," Curtis said. "I wondered why I started seeing swarms of bats flying around on winter evenings. What's the problem?"

"The bats discovered Christmas," Maq said. "I have no idea why they started obsessing about this particular human holiday. Apparently there is something about the music and bell-ringing that made the bats sentimental."

"Well," Curtis said. "I can only speak for us human beings. Here in Iowa at least, it's usually cold in December, and the days are short. It's just nice to get together with family and friends, maybe sing, and have good things to eat and drink."

"And this celebration is only for humans?" Maq asked. "Household pets enjoy Christmas," Curtis said. "Other animals end up on the menu for Christmas Day."

"So no other animals celebrate with the humans?" Maq asked.

"Not that I know of," Curtis said. "Not nowadays. I think there are various legends from the past about other animals, but I'm not big on history."

"Hmm," Maq said. "I haven't researched this holiday sufficiently. I hate to see my bats unhappy. Do you know anyone who would be willing to celebrate Christmas with bats?"

"Unlikely," Curtis said. He looked sad. "Unfortunately bats have a bad rap. People think they bite you and give you rabies or some other disease."

"That is unjust," Maq said. "The brown bats in the Maquoketa Caves consume insects. They aren't vampire bats, and they have never attacked human beings or infected any creature."

"Yeah," Curtis said. "Wasn't it the human beings who transported the fungus that gave the bats here the white-nose disease that killed so many of them?"

"Indeed," Maq said. "My bats only survived because I discovered that if I ingested a bale of roadside hemp and then ignited the digestive gas my stomach expelled, that destroyed the fungus."

"It's a shame," Curtis said. "Still, sometimes you just can't defeat ignorance and superstition. I doubt if even my relatives would celebrate Christmas with bats."

"I want my bats to be happy," Maq said. "Do you have any ideas?"

"Well," Curtis said. "There is this legend about flying reindeer transporting Santa Claus around the world in a magic sleigh to deliver presents."

"Hmm," Maq said. "I am somewhat familiar with human lore. Dragons have never actually met Santa Claus or the flying reindeer, but we creatures who aren't only of the material world don't always hang out with each other. I, for example, never had any interest in chitchat with leprechauns or sea serpents."

"Maybe you should find out if this Santa Claus exists, and if he would celebrate Christmas with your bats," Curtis said.

"Thank you for the tip," Maq said. "That sounds like a possibility."

"The story is that Santa's workshop is located at the North Pole," Curtis said. "However, the planet has been mapped thoroughly enough to say that there is no such construction at the North Pole."

"We creatures of more than one reality know how to hide if necessary," Maq said. "The legends could be accurate. Dragons generally don't bother to make themselves invisible. Our appearance often helps us get what we want. However, creatures of the magical worlds are more cautious."

"Good luck," Curtis said. "I'll be around tomorrow morning to pick up my corn liquor." The cave wall darkened.

Maq spent the rest of the morning researching Christmas festivities. Depending on planetary location, details like food, drink, and music varied. However, nowhere did any group of people mention celebrating with bats. It looked like Maq would have to seek out Santa Claus to get his bats a party.

All this mental activity wore Maq out. He was also hungry, but the need for sleep prevailed. He shut off the artificial lighting and lay down.

The bats' squeaking woke him up. They were flying around the cave.

"We'll be on our way," Bat-Out-Of-Hell said. "It's dark, and we're hungry. You usually don't sleep this long."

Maq needed a few seconds to get his brain working. "You're right," he said. "I spent a lot of time talking to Curtis about his order for corn liquor, and then I was exhausted. Thanks for waking me. I definitely need to eat. I think I'll fly north and see if I can find a tasty moose wandering around or perhaps locate a few hibernating bears in their caves for supper."

"Too rich for our taste," Bat-Out-Of-Hell said. "We'll probably just hang around the river between Green Island and Bellevue. There are still plenty of apples on the ground there. See you when we get back."

As soon as the bats left, Maq climbed up the stone steps from his residential cave, being careful to keep his balance. He had to pull his wings close to his torso to get through the rocky archways. Maq was in good shape, but even a well-toned dragon took up space. Since Maq didn't want the tourists to suspect that a dragon lived in the lower caves, he never made any changes to the entrances and exits.

Once outside in the dark, Maq spread his brawny, green wings, flapped them furiously, and rose up into the air, which was cold, but invigorating rather than unpleasant.

Maq increased his speed. Dragons actually preferred cold weather. Due to their efficient internal combustion systems, they were in danger of overheating if they spent too much time in warm environments.

Maq didn't fly this route that often, but sometimes he liked to follow the Mississippi River north to Lake Itasca. As the river narrowed, the sheets of ice covering it got wider. The trees were covered with a light layer of frost, a definite improvement over depressingly bare branches.
In the towns along the river the humans had their Christmas lighting and decorations out. Groups of humans walked from house to house and sang songs. Maq had to admit that it all felt quite festive.

No wonder the bats wanted to participate. A dragon, due to size alone, couldn't celebrate in enclosures humans found pleasant. However, little bats would have no problems flying around any party.

Flying high enough so that the humans below couldn't really see his contours, Maq puzzled over how he could help his bats.

He quickly realized that he was too hungry to think straight. One moose, two bears, four pigs later for dessert, and Maq felt satisfactorily sated.

Now Maq could indeed think clearly. He couldn't force the humans to welcome the bats. Possibly, no one could persuade humans to regard bats more kindly. That left Santa Claus. Maq flew northeast.

Curtis was correct about the legendary location. Maq located the geographical North Pole, a place in water surrounded by the cold waves of the Arctic Ocean. There were a few floating stations around the North Pole, but definitely no legendary toy factory belonging to Santa Claus.

Maq switched his vision to see the parallel, magic world. Floating above the geographical North Pole was the fabled workshop, a sparkling white, castle-like fortress constructed with bricks made out of snow. A giant sign on the top lit up in red and green proclaimed "Santa's Workshop". Eight reindeer performed various gymnastic exercises in the air above a corral next to the building while a scarlet-nosed reindeer reclining in a lounge chair on the ground barked orders.

Consistent with his nature as a courteous dragon, Maq landed at the castle gate and rang the doorbell instead of just flying into one of the larger turrets. The reindeer ignored him. To Maq's surprise, Santa himself, dressed in baggy, red pants with green suspenders and a long-sleeved, white shirt, pulled the gate open.

"Who are you, and what do you want?" the man bellowed. While Santa's belly did shake like a bowl full of jelly, he didn't laugh. His beefy, red face didn't match the visage of a kindly, old St. Nick. It occurred to Maq that he may have come at a bad time.

"Santa Claus?" Maq asked. "Sorry to bother you. I thought one of your employees would answer the door. I know how busy you are this time of year."

"The elves are busier than I am," the man said. "Tradition demands that they craft the toys themselves. Even with the help of magic, it is precision work, especially since the kids all want the latest technology."

"Should I come back later?" Maq asked. "I do need to talk to you before you start your deliveries on Christmas Eve."

"Then make it quick," Santa said. "I have to plot this year's route before I go argue with Rudolph. The reindeer always think they know better than I do, but I don't like getting lost. It's a big planet, you know."

"I just wanted to ask about how you and your employees celebrate Christmas Day, whether you could include more creatures in your festivities," Maq began.
"When we get back, all we want to do is sleep," Santa answered. "Even with magic, Christmas Eve is exhausting. The elves were working day and night all year. They need relaxation before they are back to their fun-loving selves."

Maq's wings drooped. "I understand," he said. "I hoped I could find some Christmas festivities that the bats who live in my cave could take part in. They don't hibernate anymore, my fault, and now they have discovered Christmas. The humans don't want to include bats in their celebrations. I was hoping the bats could party with you and your staff."

"Hmm," Santa said. "I see your problem, and it is admirable to want to give your bats a nice Christmas, but I can't help you. After Christmas Eve, we are all too exhausted here."

Maq's wings slumped further. "Sorry to bother you," he said to Santa. "I won't take up any more of your time. After all, Christmas Eve is next week."

"Yeah," Santa said. "That's the problem with existing in two worlds; you can't cheat space and time, even with magic."

Maq felt dejected on his flight home. Even though he hadn't yet disappointed the bats, since they knew nothing of his efforts, he wanted to make it up to them. He made a quick detour to his usual Mediterranean haunts and hauled away a few hundred pounds of tangerines and oranges for the bats.

Maq got back to his cave just after the bats, who gratefully consumed some of the citrus fruits he brought with him. They said they had flown around in the cold but hadn't found anything worth seeing, much less eating. The bats and Maq agreed that it was time to get some sleep after a strenuous night.

Maq woke up in time to greet Curtis who drove his sturdy pick-up to the lower cave door to collect his corn liquor. Maq had long since cleared a wide path from the parking lot down to the cave. Hikers in the park couldn't recognize the door to the cave, but Curtis was a steady visitor and knew how to find the entrance.

"You seem a little sad," Curtis said as he maneuvered his forklift into the lowest cave.

"I found Santa Claus," Maq said. "However, he and his crew don't celebrate Christmas. They are too tired after their work before and on Christmas Eve. Santa says they just want to end the year with sleep. So I can't get my bats a party there."

"Hmm," Curtis said as he drove the barrels to his aging truck. "I don't know the man, of course, but I wonder if you're giving up too easily. Everyone has his price. You just don't know what Santa's is."

"He exists in the magical and the material world," Maq said. "There's not much I could tempt him with."

"I don't know about your magical world," Curtis began. "However, some stuff in the material world is priceless, like your corn liquor. You should offer that to Santa."

Maq perked right up. "You might have something there," he said. "I am good at producing potables. Maybe I could get Santa to put on a party for the bats if I offered to cater it."

"If they are all as tired as Santa claims, you should start them off with some Irish coffee," Curtis said. "Enough caffeine should wake them up and keep them awake."

"Indeed," Maq said. "My Iowa whiskey has always been quite popular. I could offer Santa's crew a brunch with fortified coffee when he gets back. A boisterous party might then develop as the group consumes more of the liquids I provide. Maybe I could even persuade the elves to sing."

"I don't want to claim too much," Curtis said. "Remember, my son Cletus runs a catering business that has provided food for your social events in the past. Your dragon guests liked his food. Cletus would be happy to provide food for you to take to Santa's place. Since this is for a Christmas party, I would suggest Christmas cookies for dessert."

"Excellent," Maq said. "I'm not familiar with Christmas cookies, though. Could you bring me a few samples? All I have to do is persuade Santa Claus to let me and my bats welcome him and his employees to a brunch with Santa's Workshop. I can ask the elves to make sure it is decorated appropriately. Otherwise, I can also take care of that."

"I can't speak for magical creatures," Curtis admitted. "However, I don't know any human being who would prefer sleep to your beverages. I'll come back tomorrow, same time as today, with a few varieties of Christmas cookies, nothing exotic, just sugar cookies frosted to look Christmasy."

"Fine," Maq said. After Curtis left, Maq lay back down and slept better than ever. He had a feeling things were looking up.

That evening when the bats were getting ready to go out for brief flight of frenzy —bats being bats — Maq tried to ask indifferently just how far bats could fly.

"Fifty miles tops," Bat-Out-Of-Hell said. "At that point we have used up our energy reserves and have to gorge ourselves. Why?"

"No reason," Maq said. "I wondered if you would like to accompany me on some of my trips."

"Not unless you can transport us," Batshit Crazy said. "But bats aren't much interested in seeing the world. Eastern Iowa is enough for us."

After they left, Maq went to his computational devices and did the math. Maquoketa B. could easily transport loads of at least a hundred tons. The problem was packaging. His claws could only clutch a limited volume and things balanced on his tail or even strapped to it could fall off at high speeds. Maq needed a shipping container for the food, drinks, and bats. He could then fly that load to the North Pole.

Maq paid Santa another visit. When he opened the castle gate this time, Santa looked tired, but didn't seem as irritated as he had been before.

"Come in, but no Christmas party," Santa said before Maq could say anything. However, Maq pressed his wings together and entered the castle workshop, being careful to close the gate behind him.

Some honking and pawing noises outside increased in volume.

"Right," Maq said. "I respect that. I was wondering, though, aren't you and the reindeer hungry when you get back on Christmas morning? The bats and I would like to make a Christmas brunch for all of you. You could eat, drink, and then sleep as long as you want."

"Brunch, brunch, brunch," came a thundering chorus from outside the workshop.

"Flying reindeer are definitely too telepathically talented for their own good," Santa muttered.

He looked thoughtful. "Okay," Santa said. "We get back, consume your brunch, and then you leave, and we get to sleep. Only one condition: no damned cookies. They lay under every Christmas tree when I bring the kids their presents. I can't stand those sickeningly sweet products of obsessive bakers, but I have to eat them all. It's tradition. I feel nauseated just thinking about them."

"No problem," Maq said. "Can I get into the workshop while you are gone so I can have everything ready when you get back?"

"I'll tell the elves to wait for you," Santa said. "If you make enough noise, one of them will let you in."

Relieved, Maq flew home, taking a detour around the upper latitudes, noting where he could snatch a few decorated Christmas trees and wreaths for Santa's Workshop.

Maq returned before the bats, who then ate more oranges and tangerines and retired to get their beauty sleep at the top of the cave.

Maq set a reminder device so that he woke up before Curtis came the next morning. Maq went outside to meet him.

"The party's on," Maq said. "Or, rather, Santa has agreed to a brunch."

Curtis handed him a baking sheet with Christmas cookies, each decorated with a different seasonal designation. Since Maq hadn't had time for breakfast yet, he devoured all the cookies with one gulp. They were delicious.

"Delightful," Maq said. "Unfortunately, Santa hates cookies."

"No problem," Curtis said. "I'll tell my son to make pies instead."

"I have one more problem," Maq said. "How can I transport everything to the North Pole?"

"Right," Curtis said. "All the other parties were here in the caves. You provided the drinks, and all I had to do was deliver the food."

"Do you know where I could get a container?" Maq asked. "I'm not sure how I could get something like that transported to my cave without people noticing."

"Forget the container," Curtis said. "I drive a school bus. There is no school over the Christmas holidays. I can bring you the bus already loaded with the food, and you can borrow it. The food, drinks, and bats will have plenty of room. You just have to return it in good condition."

"Thank you," Maq said. "Perfect!"

"I'll see you on Christmas Eve," Curtis said and drove off.

When he had a clear goal in mind, Maq was able to organize everything quickly and efficiently. An examination of the brewing cave showed him that the supplies weren't sufficient, and so he got to work. A few days later, the barrels of drinks were ready to go. Maq gave Cletus a list of menu items for the party. Christmas Eve arrived. Soon after dusk, Curtis and Cletus arrived with the yellow school bus filled with containers of food. They helped Maq load the barrels of drinks into the bus and then left.

Maq climbed up to his residence cave and called the bats. They were subdued. "We don't feel like going out," Bat-In-The-Belfry said.

"I've got a surprise," Maq said. "Fly down to the brewing cave, and outside you'll see a school bus. Get on the bus, and I'll take you to your Christmas party."

He hoped he wasn't promising too much. Things could still go wrong. At this point, Maq could only hope for the best.

Maq had no problems grasping the bus and flying to Santa's Workshop. He parked the bus next to the reindeer corral and rang the doorbell but got no response.

While he was considering alternatives, the bats flew out of the bus and into the turrets while screeching loudly. Soon thereafter two elves opened the door, rubbing their eyes. It looked like they had been sleeping ever since Santa left.

"Can you get the bats to quiet down?" the first elf asked. "No problem," Maq said and waved at the bats. "We just want to fix brunch before Santa gets back. I'll get the food and drinks, and you can taste everything."

That appealed to the elves who then drank enough highly caffeinated Irish coffee to wake up. They became enthusiastic about decorating the room.

The bats got into the spirit of things, swooping up and down around the elves, who by now liked the bats. One telepathic hint from Maq, and the elves brought in musical instruments and started singing. The bats joined in, slightly off key but joyously.

When Santa arrived, the party was in full swing. The reindeer raced in and found their way to the corn liquor barrels. Santa looked annoyed.

"This isn't what I agreed to," he said. However, after several mugs of Irish coffee, he was mellow enough to sing along with the bats and elves. The snow-brick walls reverberated with a semi-accurate chorus of "We Wish You a Merry Christmas".

Some of the bats perched on the shoulders of the elves; some staggered around on the floor; some dive-bombed the liquor barrels. They all sang happily.

Santa lurched over to Maq and said, "Great food, and especially no cookies. This is better than I imagined. We'll have to do it every year from now on."

Maq was relieved. He sipped his corn liquor and smiled as he listened to his happy bats' vocals. Curtis had helped him give his bats the Merry Christmas they wanted. His next order of corn liquor would be free.

Hiraeth

By Kathryn Reilly

In dreams, they look down
witnessing the world below
every scale relishing
clouds' ephemeral caress

in dreams, they rekindle
magics lost: fire breathing,
prophecy, wish granting
shape-shifting, dream stalking

in dreams, carefully dug out dens
sparkle with golden hordes
hosting enchanted items
coveted by mages old

in dreams, humans quest:
a princess seeking freedom
a knight seeking revenge
a dragon-rider seeking endless adventure

waking, the lizards blink
hoping heat tickles their lungs

homesick, they long for the skies
but suffer sun-warmed rocks instead

they settle, waiting for their wings

Call of the Sky
By Rohan Magerman

The cold wind is my cloak
I wear it proudly as I soar
Dodging branches and high peaks
I glide to explore
Watching as our shadows touch the ground
of lands untouched by man
No sound but a crisp whisper
stillness shows all is aglow
My dragon's scales ripple from head to tail
as she wings forth toward our destination
from one mountaintop to another
without delay or hesitation
My journey is never-ending but complete
the skies my only friend and ally
no boundaries, just an open ember
where the wind sings and embraces us both
With power in our wings and strength in our bond
we sail beyond dreams and expectations
forever soaring forward to greater destinations
On a winged steed in full motion—dragon-slider true
living in this boundless flight until there's nothing left to do
but spiral up and up even higher

hearts ablaze with fervent desire
for our home that awaits in the sky.

Dragon Ground

By Oliver Smith

A king among ship-nails; in the damp clay,
his grinning skull helmed once, in dragon-green
scales and flamed dragon-gold. In the deep earth,
the dragon aches for the ponderous beat
of a drum, as the gale shrieks in the sails
and salt spray flies, all across the dark waves,

rolling as time fills the nights with the cold
ocean's booming and the hourglass sand trickles
down, through these strange storms. Like a shiver-lizard
sleeping; away the long winter, the dragon waits
down in the cold soil; sharp as a sword come fresh
from the whetstone, red as a garnet, and bright as a star.

The dragon in the earth, is wide as a kingdom
and as long as its history's threads blown
in the breath, that shakes the oaks like a hurricane,
shakes down the old kings; like November's dead
leaves, shakes granite towers; the roof, floor, and walls
built over the caverns where the old dragon sleeps;
deep under field, under greenwood, under village
and farm; spine under highland, flanks under

lowland, and head resting out in the sea. Under
stones, under rock, living root, and dead bone.
Its claws hold this hall, this brick house, this old castle,
this hovel, this palace of marble, this green grove,
this homeland grown restless and wild. The dragon's
dream buried in the whisper of legends; or carved
coiled like serpents around the church door;
or rearing up proud at the prow of a warship;
now rising on wings of turbulent brimstone
woken from under the long-barrow mound.

Dragons, Damsels, and Danish Pastries

By L N Hunter

'Right, off you go then.' The sergeant gave the young woman a shove with the butt of his spear and backed away from the cave entrance.

Iphigenia turned to glare at him tight-lipped, but he refused to meet her gaze, instead staring intently at a point somewhere over her shoulder. She straightened her back, sniffed haughtily and marched across the final patch of grass, but tripped over the hem of her overlong white dress. Fortunately, her hands had been tied in front of her rather than behind, so the main damage when she fell was to her pride. She picked herself up, awkwardly attempting to wipe the dirt from the dress that had been made specially—and hastily—for the occasion, and strode into the darkness of the cave entrance.

'Oi,' she called. 'Dragon, are you in here? Well, come on, get it over with. I'm your sacrifice and I hope you damned well choke on me!'

A gust of hot air fluttered her hair, and a red glow appeared from beyond a bend in the depths of the cave.

The blood drained from Iphigenia's face. She gulped, her bravado shrivelling into a solid lump before plummeting to the bottom of her stomach. She thought about making a run for it, but knew that was out of the question. If she didn't continue into the cave, the village would be razed to the ground, and everyone in it—including herself—would be killed.

She couldn't stop herself from wondering what it would feel like to be burned to a crisp. *I hope it'll be quick.* The thought brought tears to her eyes as she forced her legs to take her towards the source of the fiery glow. When she turned the corner into a wide chamber, she stopped and let out a gasp.

The glow came from a log-fired oven from which a tray of pastries was being extracted. Iphigenia couldn't help but notice that the hand holding the tray was scaly, green and equipped with claws.

The owner of the hand was roughly twice human-size, with a long, lizard-like face atop a sinuous neck and a pair of leathery wings. Its other, equally green, equally clawed hand held a spatula. An arrow-tipped tail flicked into view between the legs of the stool it perched on.

The creature's slit-pupiled eyes blinked, and it smiled. Iphigenia's world shrank to the bright array of dagger-sharp teeth until the dragon broke the spell by speaking.

'Don't just stand there, my dear. I've been waiting for you. Something to eat?' The dragon gestured with its spatula towards a table holding a tea service, several plates of neatly trimmed sandwiches and assorted pastries, and a bottle of wine. 'Or a nice cuppa? Is it just you, or is anyone else coming?'

Iphigenia's brow furrowed as her mind raced. She asked, 'Is this some sort of grotesque game before you eat me?'

The dragon set down the tray of freshly baked apple turnovers and turned towards her. 'Eat you? Why would I do that?'

'But isn't that why I'm here? Smoke coming from the top of the mountain, polite but menacing letter delivered to the mayor requesting prompt delivery of damsels to the cave— this cave. Can't be any more obvious than that.' She waved her bound hands towards herself as best she could. 'So here I am. But don't think you'll get away with it! Knights are already on their way to avenge me.'

The dragon scowled and smoke plumed from its nostrils. 'Bloody knights. What is it with you lot and knights?' Iphigenia shrank back as it thrust the spatula at her. 'Many a time, there I am, minding my own business, staring at clouds and listening to birdsong, when suddenly, knights! Pointing their whatchamacallums, lances, at me and shouting, "Have at thee, vile wyrm." And then, because I have the audacity to jump out of the way, the drama queens leap off their horses and come at me, waving their swords like overexcited toddlers with new toys.' The dragon waved its spatula like such a sword. 'I ask you, what's a dragon supposed to do?' Iphigenia snapped, 'Well, if you didn't demand damsels, we wouldn't send knights to attack you!'

The dragon's jaw dropped. 'But I'm just being polite. It's awkward when you're new to town. The incumbents can be so suspicious of strangers, so I thought that a tea party for the ladies and some sort of friendly sporting event for the menfolk would break the ice. I don't know what sort of sports are popular around here, so I figured on asking the women when they arrived. But what do I get instead? Just one unfriendly girl, and the threat of yet more knights.'

Its lips trembled, and its eyes started to glisten. 'I'm going to have to move again, aren't I? I've only just got this place the way I like it.'

It dropped the spatula and put its head in its hands. A pang of guilt hit Iphigenia. She went to the dragon, and after a nervous hand-hover, awkwardly stretched up to pat its shoulder——the scales were smoother than she expected, not stiff and unyielding. 'There, there. I'm sure it's not all that bad. You're a Gods-damned *dragon* after all.'

The dragon wailed, 'It's just not fair.'

Iphigenia clumsily extracted a lace handkerchief from the sleeve of her dress and handed it to the crying dragon. She crossed to the table and poured two cups of tea. 'Come over here. Let's have a drink, and you can tell me all about it.'

Watching the dragon blow its nose, she decided she probably didn't want the now sticky and slightly charred hankie back, even though the embroidery was some of her best work. She sipped her tea while she waited for the creature to compose itself.

Eventually, it shook its shoulders, wrapped both hands around the cup and stared into it. It grumbled, 'Frogs get kissed by princesses; mermaids get their princes, not to mention a free pair of legs. Even Beast ended up with a nice wife and a makeover. Humans fawn over unicorns, but what about me, eh? All I ever see are screaming villagers and homicidal knights. And they usually end up screaming, too.

I'm a majestic mythical creature, and everyone wants me dead.'

'I'm sure it's not that bad…'

'Oh yeah, you think? Things were great up until about three thousand years ago. In China, you humans *worshipped* us. Then, just one teeny-weeny little accident with the Emperor's son, and that was the end. He had plenty of other sons, so why get so worked up about this one? Do shepherds worry about one little sheep out of their flocks? I mean, it's—'

'Actually, they do. Every lamb is important.'

The dragon blinked. 'Really? But you eat them.'

'Well… Hang on, are you implying that you consider humans a source of food?'

'Uh, um…' The dragon glanced away. 'No, not at all. Not now. Maybe in the distant past, before we knew better. We didn't distinguish between all you mammals. Soz.'

Iphigenia absentmindedly picked up an apple danish.

'Oh, do help yourself, my dear. Wait, let me get that for you.'

Before she could react, the dragon had swiped a claw through the rope binding her hands. Once her heart had stopped hammering at the sight of the razor-sharp claw missing her skin by a hairsbreadth, Iphigenia rubbed her wrists and mumbled, 'Thanks.'

The dragon's lips turned down. 'Shame nobody else bothered to turn up. I spent all morning baking, and for what? Just one skinny girl.'

'Hey, who're you calling skinny? You're a bit of a shrimp for a mighty dragon, yourself!'

'I'm small because I haven't been eating well—it's not my fault.'

It smiled, and Iphigenia shrank back from the dazzling teeth.

'Oh, look, I'm sorry,' the dragon said. 'Nobody likes dragons. I blame bloody Heracles. After China, we moved to the Mediterranean. That was pleasant—lovely blue sea, miles of beaches. Human and dragon living together. But then Heracles came along with his sodding twelve labours. I ask you, how ridiculous is the idea of giant dogs, bulls, boar and all the rest?' It threw its hands into the air. 'They were *all* dragons. He really didn't like having us around and set about eliminating all of us. We weren't even eating humans by that stage—well, not many.'

The dragon thumped the table, spilling some of the cup of tea and startling Iphigenia.

'It's just not fair. Bloody humans. Why do I bother?' Smoke drifted from its nostrils again.

Iphigenia thought she'd better distract the dragon. 'We haven't been properly introduced yet. My name's Iphigenia. Iphigenia Penelope Heppelthwaite. But you can call me Effie—all my friends do.' She did a sort of seated half-curtsy.

The smoke subsided, and the dragon said, 'Friends—are we…? I haven't been able to call anyone a friend for centuries.' It bowed. 'Pleased to meet you, Effie. My full name is Dracona Behofnungiskranticaldera Hyphonicastigon, but you can call me Callie.'

Iphigenia pursed her lips. 'Callie, that's a nice name. I wonder if I could ask a personal question…'

The dragon raised an eyebrow.

'Are you—this is awfully embarrassing—male or female?' Iphigenia had assumed that the dragon must be male, what with the damsels and so on, but the ending of 'Dracona' as well as the name 'Callie' made her think that perhaps she was mistaken. 'I do apologise if that's overly intrusive.'

'Oh, dragons don't do all that complicated business of him with the dangly bits and her with the, you know'—the dragon gestured with its hands in front of its chest—'the bumps on the front.' We're whatever gender we want to be, whenever we want to be.'

Iphigenia thought the matter over for a moment. 'But then, how do you, um, reproduce?'

Callie leaned its head back and laughed. A burst of flame escaped its mouth, singeing the cave's ceiling and making Iphigenia flinch.

'Oh, my dear, there are so few of us around that we couldn't possibly rely on pairing up. No, when the time is right, we spontaneously ignite and spawn offspring from the ashes. Have you heard of the phoenix?' Without waiting for an answer, Callie continued, 'More Greek lies. It's a description of a dragon, not a bird.'

'But that must mean the parent… er… dies.'

Callie shrugged. 'The memories live on in our offspring, who add their own experiences to pass on to the next generation. I'm physically only a hundred and twenty, but I can remember the siege of Troy and the construction of the pyramids.'

'Wow!' A thought struck Iphigenia, and she added, 'How come no one knows this?'

Callie gave her a look. 'After Heracles and the rest, what human has ever paid attention to anything a dragon *says*? You're all too busy screaming and running away or waving swords and running towards us.'

Iphigenia settled into her chair and picked up another pastry—a maple pecan plait this time. She took a bite, and with a sigh, said, 'This is heavenly. Anyone would think you're fattening me up, ready to eat.'

Callie snapped, 'Don't even joke about that!'

Iphigenia set the half-eaten pastry on her plate. 'Sorry.' Callie rested its head on the table. 'Oh, it's not your fault. I'm no good with people. I try, but all the screaming and shouting… I don't get a lot of practice at simply talking.'

Iphigenia chewed her lip. 'Sit up, Callie. We're talking now. Tell me something… I know, tell me about gold—is it true that dragons have lots of treasure?'

'Pah, as if!' Callie waved a hand around. 'Would I be living in a cave like this if I had treasure?'

'Oh. More dragon misinformation?'

'No, it's all to do with spawning. That needs a lot of energy—an awful lot of energy. We can live quite happily on just one sheep or… the like'—Iphigenia was pretty sure Callie meant humans—'per week, but when we're ready to ignite, we need much more. As many as a hundred sheep. Ha, I remember one of my ancestors ate so many mammoths, they went extinct. But that's rather inefficient—takes ages to catch that many animals who don't especially want to be eaten, and takes almost as long to consume them.' The dragon patted its stomach. 'Really puts a strain on the lower intestine, too.

No, our ancestors discovered that metal was a much better source of energy than carbon. Say, you don't know if there's any gold around here?'

'Gold?'

'Oh, never mind. Seems to be something only a few humans have in quantity—I don't really understand why, since it's not very useful to you. So, dragons who want offspring would collect the equivalent of a few hundred sheep in gold, consume it, and then: bang! Flames, noise, baby dragons.'

Iphigenia grimaced and reached for another pastry. 'Iron's acceptable too, though not as good as gold. The one nice thing about knights is all that armour they insist on wearing.'

Iphigenia paled, then changed the subject. 'What about you? Any plans to…' She lifted her hands and pulled them apart in an explosion sort of gesture.

Callie shook its head. 'No, not ready yet. Can't get into the right frame of mind. I wouldn't want to pass on my miserable memories to a bunch of babies.' It sighed. 'No, I need to find something to make me happy so I can pass on a worthwhile legacy.'

'Maybe I can help.' Iphigenia's voice faltered. 'No, wait, that sounds like I want you to die.'

Callie chuckled. 'I must say, I've not smiled so much in decades. You're a nice person for a human.'

'So, what would make you happy?'

'A quiet, comfortable life. With a few sheep and some friends. Then, eventually, enough gold to spawn.'

Iphigenia pulled at her lower lip. She cast her eyes about the chamber, until her gaze landed on the plates of baked goods.

'I've got an idea… Dad's the village baker, and I can tell you he'd be proud to have danishes like these in his shop. Maybe you could, um, do some work for us, making pastries.' She snapped her fingers 'I know! You could help out at the blacksmith's as well—he's always complaining about how difficult it is to keep his forge hot. We could show everyone that you're a good egg, and they'd pay you in sheep or scrap metal.'

'But they'd still just look on me as a monster and run screaming.'

'Maybe initially, but we just need to work on presenting a positive image. Look, I'll take some of these pastries back with me. I won't tell people where they came from, but I know they'll love them. I'll come back to work on our marketing strategy, and collect more of your baking. It won't be long before people will be begging for more pastries, and then I'll bring a few villagers out here to meet you.'

Callie tapped its teeth with the tip of a claw, making a disconcerting clicking sound which Iphigenia tried to ignore.

'We might have to work on your presentation,' she said. 'Tone down the teeth and the fire and the whole eating people thing.'

'Oh, it's never going to work.'

Iphigenia patted Callie's arm again.

'It'll just take a little time. As soon as the villagers taste your baking, they'll be desperate for more. And once you take charge of the forge, the smith will make better weapons than anyone in the area.'

Callie scowled. 'Weapons for knights.'

'Well, maybe. But the villagers would keep them from bothering you—you'd be an asset to us. Anyway, sometimes the village needs weapons to protect us from our enemies.'

Callie gave a tentative smile.

'Enemies—you mean other humans? Would your village folk mind if I ate some of them?'

Iphigenia gulped. 'It depends. Maybe. People tend to be a bit touchy about things like that. Anyway, there's other stuff you could do—say, fly overhead and scare them away instead of killing them.'

'I suppose I can give it a try. What have I got to lose? If I'm going to be hounded out of my home, at least this'll delay things for a bit.'

'Come on, it's not that bad. Now, have you got a box or something for a few of these delights?'

Just as Callie stood up, a shout came from outside. 'Ho there, vile wyrm! Come out and meet your doom at the swords of the Knights of Justice and Humanity.'
'Oh, for fff....' Callie hissed, smoke billowing from its nostrils, engulfing the chamber and making Iphigenia's eyes water.

She coughed, and spluttered, 'No wait, Callie. Don't do it. I'll go out and calm them down.'
Callie stopped smoking instantly, and the fumes cleared rapidly.

I suppose it makes sense that a creature who can create fire would have efficient ventilation, Iphigenia thought. *Maybe Callie can help with house design, too.*

She strode out of the cave carrying a plate of pastries, and confronted five hulking knights seated on five enormous horses.

'Have at thee, vile—" the leader started. "Wait, you're not a dragon, are you?'

Iphigenia smiled sweetly. 'How astute of you. There're no dragons here. Just me and my secret bakery.'
She followed the knight's eyes to the smoke wafting from the cave.

'Oh, I burned the last batch. Ha, serves me right for getting caught up in my maidenly needlework and not paying attention to the oven. You know how addled us helpless girls get.'

The knight attempted to scratch his head, but bumped his gloved fingers against his helmet.

'So… You're certain there are no dragons here?'

Iphigenia looked left and right, exaggeratedly craning her neck. 'Nope, not a single one. I'm afraid you've been mustered under false pretences.' She held up the plate. 'Would you care for something sweet?'

One of the knights stretched an arm out, but the leader of the group snapped, 'Oh, for pity's sake. Right, lads, about face. Back to the village. Lucky we've got that clause in the contract about our non-refundable callout fee.'

The knight who'd been reaching for a danish looked disappointed, but obeyed his commander's order.

Iphigenia called out, 'Drop by the village bakery during your lunch break. We'll have more pastries.'

She watched the knights disappear into the distance, then called over her shoulder, 'You can come out now.'
Callie stepped out, scowling in the direction of the departing knights, its tail swishing irritably.

'There, that was easy, wasn't it?' Iphigenia said.
Callie harrumphed and stomped back into the cave.
Iphigenia smiled. 'Oh, you old grump! Give it a chance. You'll be part of our little community in no time.'